Stewards of Octarma and the Cosmic Realm of the Gas Giants

GW01057441

Output 1.0

R. H. Polden

National Library of Australia Cataloguing-in-Publication entry:
Creator: Polden, R.H., author.
Title: Stewards of Octarma and the Cosmic Realm of the Gas Giants: Stewards of Octarma Book One
ISBN: 9780645486063 (Paperback)
Subjects: Science Fiction/Humour Novella.

Tale Publishing
Melbourne Victoria

Tale

Dedication

To my father, RIP.

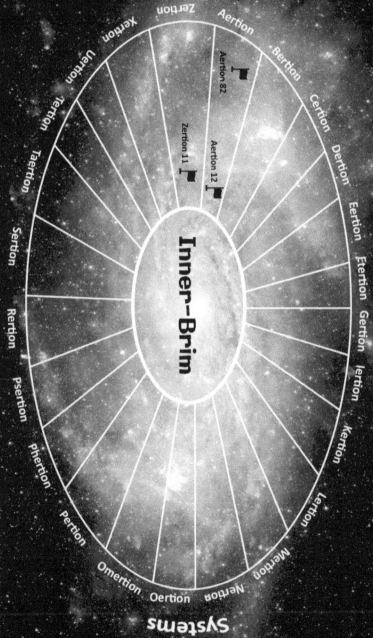

Subrium Universe Tourism Board
Qurkition Galaxy

Outer-Brim

Systems

Outer-Brim

Inner-Brim

Aertion
Bertion
Certion
Dertion
Eertion
Etertion
Gertion
Iertion
Kertion
Lertion
Mertion
Nertion
Oertion
Omertion
Pertion
Phertion
Psertion
Rertion
Sertion
Taertion
Tertion
Uertion
Xertion
Zertion

Aertion 82
Aertion 12
Zertion 11

1. The Milarum Family

"BOIL ME AN EGG! I WILL BE BACK TO CRACK IT!"

Aertion 82 was a desolate planet, with little to keep the average tourist happy, unless of course they loved amusing themselves with dirt. With no indigenous population to speak of, the only object of any significance was a huge high-rise building — the third largest in the Qurkition galaxy — which sat right in the middle of Aertion 82's largest continent.

At just over two thousand storeys high and made from solid nano-carbon, this impressive building sparkled in the bright early-sun-cycle sunlight, like the beacon of enlightenment it was designed to represent. It had once been home to the most powerful men in Qurkition, who in theory, used it as a meeting place to discuss important galactic issues. However, in practice, it only ended up serving as a place for these so called 'powerful men' to crash after a hard night-cycle on the booze.

It was therefore a joyous sun-cycle[1] for the many wives of these pointless men, when Miss Felicity Milarum, the CEO of the galaxy's largest children's entertainment corporation, It's All For Effect (IAFE), swept in and bought the entire planet, and shut down the boys' club in the process. She appointed her two Felecrins[2], Matilda and Fredrick, to the board of directors, and

---

[1] A sun-cycle, also known by the great unwashed, as simply a day. A single cycle equates to around a twentieth of a sun-cycle. But often lazy locals interchange the word sun-cycle with simply cycle just to keep other lazy locals on their toes (if they have them). A lunar-cycle is around 35 sun-cycles, and a solar-cycle is around 10 lunar-cycles. A flash is a second, and a moment is a minute but can sometimes feel longer. It is all frightfully interesting if you're into that sort of thing. Or if you are of a non-clean nature.

[2] Imagine a kitten and a bunny combined into one highly intelligent, cuddly-yet-deadly fluff ball.

2

turned the entire building into her corporate headquarters.

It was in this very same building that Nickolas Milarum[3], on being summoned to a meeting with his older sister Felicity, had detoured via his favourite bar, The Singing Sausage[4], for a few stiff drinks beforehand. This also gave Nickolas ample time to reminisce with his fellow patrons about his previous adventures — whether the patrons fancied the idea or not.

"Prepare to get the ship as close to the planet's surface as possible computer! I am going in! I am going in all pistols blazing! I shouted as I sat in the cockpit of my spacecraft, as it twisted and turned violently to evade the haze of laser fire and massive explosions all around," Nickolas said to the crowd of people around him while he sipped on his twelfth cocktail, aptly named, The-Singing-Bullshit-Artist[5].

"Oh, put a sock in it," came a call from the crowd.

Nickolas went on regardless. "No, my High Muck-a-muck!

---

[3] Nickolas Milarum — according to his dating profile (as annotated by the Qurkition Law Enforcement Bureau (QLEB) Romance Scam division):
Age: A young at heart 29 solar-cycles. QLEB: 35 solar-cycles.
Race: Humanoid Plus. QLEB: Humanoid — awaiting confirmation.
Occupation: Intergalactic Man of Mystery. QLEB: Children's Entertainer.
Height and Build: Well above average. Some would say muscle bound. QLEB: Average, and out of shape.
Eyes: A beautiful emerald green. QLEB: Green.
Hair: Magnificent. QLEB: Brown.
Credit Rating: Amazing. QLEB: In the toilet.
Hobbies: Long walks along the beach, charity work. QLEB: Drinking, gambling, and destroying planets.
Interesting Fact: Voted the most likely to succeed by everyone he has ever met.
QLEB: Voted the most likely to get shot if his old school master ever sees him again.

[4] It also happened to be the only pub on the planet that Nickolas wasn't barred from.

[5] The-Singing-Bullshit-Artist Cocktail ingredients:
6 shots whisky
1 shot fruity-flavoured soft drink
Splash of Bitters.
Ice.
Place ice in a glass. Add whisky. Add soft drink. Sprinkle on the Bitters. Imbibe.
Rinse and Repeat. This cocktail stimulates the bullshit centre of the imbiber's brain, diabolical story-telling, and bad karaoke without the music.

It's way too dangerous on the planet's surface. It's a way one ticket to oblivion,' replied my ship's computer, as I—"

"Do a voice you twat. None of this 'replied my computer' rubbish."

"That may be, computer. But those eight princesses held hostage—"

"It was only six earlier!"

"'Oh! Please, High Muck-a-muck! Don't go! You're the biggest deal in the universe, a hero's hero!' replied my ship's computer."

"Voice!" this was shouted in an ominous tone.

"Yes, I know I am. Nevertheless, I must go. Those cute chicks need me!"

Some of Nickolas' audience shook their heads and rolled their eyes, others moved to the other end of the long bar, hoping to be out of earshot. Still undeterred, Nickolas continued his tale.

"Time for this hero to take a break from standing still. It's GO time! I shouted as I swooped down from lower orbit and skimmed the planet's surface. So long, computer! Boil me an egg! I will be back to crack it! I shouted as I activated my transport system and teleported to the planet's surface."

"Okay. That's about enough Milarum," the bar manager said, as Nickolas had not only lost his audience, but some had threatened to become rather hostile towards him. "Although, I'm quite impressed you kept a straight face when spinning us your latest steaming pile of bullshit."

"What? Doesn't anyone want to know how I saved the princesses?" Nickolas looked around, trying to make eye contact with anyone, including the cleaning droids.

"Not particularly. I would like to know how you intend on settling your bill though."

"Oh, yeah. Well, here's the thing—"

"That's okay, my jolly barkeep. I will settle my twin's tab," said a voice from behind Nickolas. It was Jonathan who'd entered the drinking establishment only a few moments earlier.

"If that is the case then, one more for the road," Nickolas said, not even looking up.

"Bar's closed," the bar manager said, as he started processing the credit chip that Jonathan had handed him. "And if you two are twins, then I'm queen of the entire universe[6]."

Nickolas half fell from his bar stool while struggling to put on his large black coat. "Cheerio then, your Highness."

"Oh, I see what you did there. Very witty," the manager replied. "And as a reward for your loyal patronage this cycle, you're barred from The Singing Sausage, Milarum. For life!"

"Yes, indeed," Jonathan said. "Point taken, old bean. It's time for us to be toddling off anyway."

Jonathan grabbed his brother before he could take a swing at the bar manager, "This little detour of yours has probably kept Felicity waiting, which is never a good thing."

"Oh, happy sun-cycles!" Nickolas said as the brothers left the bar, entered a nearby Assist-o-Lift[7], scanned their security credentials, and pressed the button for the top floor.

"Yes, indeed they are 'happy sun-cycles.' We haven't seen Felicity in jolly well ages. I'm looking forward to it. I wonder what this is all about."

---

[6] Obviously, the barkeep is ignorant of the phenomenon of fraternal twins.

[7] The new sensation in multi-tasking lift technology, the Assist-o-Lift performs all the functions of both a traditional lift and personal assistant. This included assisting managers when they required staff to consider pursuing other career opportunities — achieved by sacking staff to the smooth tunes of elevator music while it whizzed the poor sods to the basement where security awaited them. A little wonder that since they were installed, there has never been an issue catching lifts, as 99% of the staff use the stairs.

"Nothing good I bet. Probably wants to fire us in person."

The lift found its landing floor, informed them that Felicity would be along shortly and opened its doors directly into her office. The room was packed with massive computer displays, large leather couches, bookcases jam-packed with electronic documents, and enough priceless ancient artefacts to put most museums to shame.

"Us or you?" Jonathan said as he made himself comfortable on one of the couches.

Nickolas meanwhile rummaged through the ridiculously large bar fridge on the far wall, looking for a stiff drink. "Oh, and thanks for rumbling my fun back there. Another few moments and I would have had that entire drinking-pit eating out of my hands." To his dismay he found only large bottles of plain water, larger bottles of water with lemon, and the usual variations of frightfully expensive water substitutes.

"Indeed. Curse on me for paying your tab and breaking up the jolly good time you were obviously having. What was it again? Boil me an egg, I will be back sometime to crack-up?" Jonathan laughed. "You've obviously been watching way too many late-night-cycle entertainment modules of *Smash Buffhack: Space Adventurer*."

"Bugger off, you posh git. Although come to think of it, conning barkeeps is probably the most interesting thing to do on this planet anyway."

"I would tend to agree with you, old bean. Aertion 82 is probably the dreariest planet in the entire Aertion System."

"Don't get me wrong," Nickolas said, who was at best only half listening to his brother, while still rummaging through the H2O-only enabled bar in the vain hope water would turn into a form of rocket fuelled cocktail. "I do enjoy catching the breeze with the Felecrins and staring aimlessly at the endless piles of worthless sand this planet is made up of. However, if I stay here any longer than a sun-cycle or so, there's the distinct possibility I might be bored to death."

Nickolas gave up on the fridge and searched a nearby bookcase for any sign of a fermented anything, hoping it may have lost its the way to the fridge, and instead hidden itself within a random book[8].

"Oh, don't worry *dearest* brother," came a sudden voice from behind Nickolas. "When you do eventually die, I will freeze you in ice until a cure is found. Hopefully, one sun-cycle is all they will require to solve the riddle that has perplexed every scientist in the galaxy — of how so much crap can fit into such a little numpty-brain like yours. In the meantime, please do me the honour of getting your grubby hands off my expensive furniture."

Felicity casually strolled across the room and plonked herself in her favourite chair, positioned right behind a centre console that controlled around two hundred screens. "Perhaps a few cycles off the sauce might do you some good Nickolas and would probably cost me less too. I mean, in between compensating the planet you did your last children's performance on, and the whole Zertion 11 business, it's almost more profitable to pay top credits to have you two disappear ... Permanently."

"A little harsh, old girl, don't you think?" Jonathan said.

"But I do blame you, Jonathan Oliver Milarum. You, being the more sensible of the two, should know better than to let

---

[8] This is not as odd as you might think. The tragedy of the Adams family on Dertion 3 was well known. It all started when Mrs Adams started purchasing their weekly grocery shopping from the new 'smart-enabled' hypermarket. Things kicked off promising with a pound of butter assisting the youngest child with her maths homework. However, it did eventually end in tears when the 'smart food', which didn't fancy being eaten, took to hiding throughout the house. Eventually the entire family starved to death while trying to find the sentient food.

yourself get tangled up in the chaos your brother here tends to jump headfirst into."

"Quite. Nonetheless, please consider the trouble I most definitely keep him out of. But, yes, I will try harder to keep him from mischief in the future." Jonathan knew better than to argue.

"Not likely," Nickolas replied, "It wasn't my fault Beeksy didn't know the tricks and I had to go to Plan B. At least I didn't need to use my trusty EITD[9]."

Jonathan shook his head. He knew what was coming.

"What Plan B? … Who's Beeksy? … You know what? … I don't want to know, but let me remind you morons that this planet, or any planet for that matter, doesn't take too kindly to their children being subjected to one of your famous 'Plan Bs' or transported somewhere random via your little gizmo[10]," Felicity shouted.

"And as far as that 'Zertion 11 business' is concerned …" Nickolas continued undeterred, "Ancient history."

"It was two sun-cycles ago!" Felicity shook her head as she brought up a screen showing the result of their latest handy work. One brother felt a slight pang of guilt as they looked at a planet slowly breaking in half.

"The Overlord did want us to 'illuminate proceedings' when he engaged our services," Jonathan added, in Nickolas' defence.

"Yes, however, he was probably thinking more along the lines of waking up in the early-sun-cycle with a massive hangover and four traffic cones in his bed. Not waking up to find half his planet disintegrated and nothing to show for it but a big fat bill. Lucky the sector's authorities consider what you did as a service to the community. Given its population's dubious reputation." It

---

[9] Emergency Intergalactic Transport Device (EITD).

[10] Except of course Lertion 3 where children were universally frowned upon.

wasn't lost on Felicity that no matter what sticky situation her brothers got into, they always seemed to squirm their way out of it.

Nickolas shrugged. "Meh. Either way, both incidents weren't my fault. Anyway, moving right along, I should thank you for inviting us to your lovely empty planet. I'm sure our grandmother, rest her soul, would be proud of the way you have grown her business from the small and caring 'a child's smile is worth all the credits in the galaxy' company, into the ruthless corporate machine it is now. But I'm sure the policy of ruling the family empire with an iron fist is in the original company's charter somewhere … so, good job, sis." Nickolas sat and took the shortest drink possible from his non-alcoholic beverage, while making the face of a man who had been poisoned.

"All I will say is this … when our 'friends' on what's left of Zertion 11 finally catch up with you, as indeed they will, I'll have no problem thinking up a thoughtful gravestone caption for you. *Nickolas Milarum. It was NEVER his fault.*"

"Whatever happens, they will never take my brother alive. Guaranteed or your credits back," Nickolas said, as he glanced at Jonathan and winked.

"Enough of this reminiscing. As much as I treasure our little family get-togethers, let's get down to the reason why I requested your presences."

The lights dimmed, and a very large virtual screen appeared in the middle of the office.

"Three sun-cycles ago, I received a package from one of our father's personal couriers. I tried to contact Daddy but have been unable to find him on the last planet he was sighted on. Or on any other planet for that matter. He has even switched off the personal tracking device I told him never to turn off, and I'm beginning to fear he's been kidnapped, or worse."

Felicity de-encrypted the communication module she'd received and played it on the screen.

"My dear children, I don't have much time, so I will make this expeditious" — Oliver Milarum, the Milarum children's father, looked a little nervous — "as I think I'm being followed, hence this communication. Let me begin. Firstly, Felicity, please give the item I sent with this communication to Xymod."

As instructed, Felicity stood up, removed a package from her console's top drawer, walked across the room and handed it to a tall, thin, slightly pale gent with long black hair wearing a sharp white suit who'd seemingly appeared out of thin air.

Nickolas almost fell off his chair in surprise. "Where the hell did he come from?"

"I've been here all along." Xymod smiled. "Good to see you both. Now, what do we have here?" He slowly unwrapped the package and examined the item inside.

As he held it up, the Milarum children studied the object themselves. It was a star-shaped Amulet, made from a material unknown to them, with tiny jewels encrusted around its edges, and three empty diamond-shaped slots, which surrounded a magnificent black jewel in the centre.

At Xymod's touch, the jewels embedded in the Amulet illuminated, and an astonishing multi-coloured light burst from the Amulet and danced around the room. The light was so pure, so powerful, that for a split flash it seemed as though the entire universe was a much smaller place.

A moment later, the light was gone.

Xymod stared at the Amulet intensely, his face pale, his arms shaking.

"It's all right, old friend," continued the voice of Oliver

Milarum, "I promised you when we purchased this planet I would find the Amulet for you some sun-cycle. Then again, I get the feeling that it found me. But that is a story for another time. Felicity knows who you are and how important you are to the entire Qurkition galaxy, my friend, my teacher."

Xymod nodded and continued to stare at the Amulet in almost disbelief.

"My children. As per the legend, take this Amulet and visit each of the three legendary Octarma planets. Xymod knows where they are. Find each of the three Shards — Lux, Materia and Vigor — known more commonly as Light, Matter, and Energy. Once you have located and fused the Shards back into the Amulet, harness its immense power and destroy the Black Mist, which has now been sighted in Qurkition. Lore has foretold that the Black Mist has been searching planets for the Octarm Amulet, and the Ancient Order of the Octarma, who have protected it for eons.

"Be warned, many will try to stop you. An evil force, the Zarnegy, fanatical disciples of Victarm, control the Black Mist itself. With the Black Mist now sighted close to the Aertion System, the Mist could already have commenced scanning planets for any sign of the Amulet or Shards. Make no mistake, the Zarnegy are a cruel and ruthless race who won't stop until they gain control of the Amulet.

"Lastly to you, my children. I know I wasn't always there for you while you were growing up. Too busy being a fool and chasing a fool's dream. I beg you to put aside your differences, and continue this quest for me, your mother, and our galaxy. I fear we are all in grave danger. There is no time to—"

"Stop transmission!" Nickolas spat as he jumped to his feet. "No time! All right! No time to complete your 'quest' at being possibly the worst father ever[11]. So let me get this straight. The old bugger wants us to find some mythical Shards that obviously don't exist from planets in the galaxy. Then use this Amulet to protect us from an impending deadly force we know nothing about, all the while keeping an eye out for whatever knows what. I mean, the entire universe knows the bedtime story of *Octarm and Victarm: Custodians of the Universe.* Octarm, the guardian of light, and Victarm, the nasty piece of work. Yak, yak, yak ..."

"I mean, wouldn't it be easier if I nip down to any one of our twenty-five million children's toy factory outlets, pick up the entire replica Octarm Amulet of Light boxset, along with the bonus set of Black Mist-themed steak knives, and put the worst kept secret in the universe out of its misery once and for all?"

Nickolas believed his father had not only lost a few marbles by this time, but obviously it was the entire bag, along with his mind.

"Can I stop you there, brother," Felicity interjected, "for no other reason than I want you to shut it, and seriously consider a long career in silent analysis."

At this point Xymod strode into the centre of the room, and for a moment it felt to everyone as though all the energy of the planet flowed through him. When he spoke, it seemed like he was somehow from another time. "Everything your father has

---

[11] Public records indicate this assessment was close. However, the worst father in the history of the galaxy was Noojkillo Quoopo of Pertion 13, who sold his children into slavery to buy shares in a nearby salt mine that he had a hunch was going to strike gold. He trusted that his return on investment would be so great, that not only could he buy his kids back (before his wife figured out what had happened) but also turn a tidy profit to boot. Unfortunately, the salt mine not only failed to discover gold, but it also ran out of salt. His wife, learning sometime later of his misguided business venture (it was obvious her children weren't in boarding school after all) decided to turn a nice little profit herself by selling Noojkillo to the Astro-Herders on the Outer-Brim. The last time anyone heard of Noojkillo, he was counting pebbles in the largest astro field in the galaxy.

said is true. *Wise it is to comprehend the whole*. The Octarm Amulet does exist."

"Now with all due respect, Xymod," Nickolas said, "I know you are one strange and learned fellow, even though at times you seem to be one walking and talking random cryptic proverb generator. However, how do you know this nonsense isn't simply the ramblings of an old man?"

"Because I am one. I am what your father said. I am an Octarma."

Nickolas looked at Xymod suspiciously. "Great. One Shard found and we haven't even left the office."

"Unfortunately, not. I don't have one myself. My brothers do."

"Okay," Nickolas said, "so maybe those cocktails earlier did finally kill the last of my brain cells. Because to my way of thinking if you are an Octarma and the Octarma have the Shards, then shouldn't you have one?"

"I am a Collector. My brothers and their planets, who shelter the Shards, are the Keepers. My task is to assemble the Amulet, but only when it senses impending danger and presents itself. That is the prophecy. That is why I think it made itself available to your father."

"Oh … then why didn't you say that in the beginning? It seems so obvious now. And in light of your overwhelming evidence, I have to agree with everything you said. Well argued, my friend!" Nickolas said sarcastically, as he sat down, shaking his head. "It's obviously 'believe in an ancient feeble fable cycle' and someone neglected to send me the interoffice transmission."

"I don't care about what you believe, Nickolas James Milarum." Felicity shouted, as she launched out of her chair and stared him in the face. "There won't be any long discussions, workshops or family meetings of the minds here. If Daddy has asked us to investigate, it's simple. You, your much more sensible brother, and I, are going to investigate. So, before you try to worm out of this, little brother," she continued in a pitch that would make a screaming banshee proud, "let me remind you of all the times this fine company YOUR family built with THEIR own hands has bailed you out of all your misadventures. It's extremely simple, gentlemen. After countless wasted cycles, while occasionally attempting to entertain young children or blasting them into outer space, it's time for you to step up, contribute, and bring value. Yes, my dear brothers, it's time for you to be actually useful."

The room fell silent. Jonathan, who, up to now, had been keeping his thoughts to himself, stood, walked over to Felicity and put his hand on her shoulder. "Count me in, Felicity. Of course, I will help. Family is family after all, and who knows what the old boy has got himself mixed up in this time."

Nickolas, on the other hand, wasn't so forthcoming. He looked about as enthusiastic as someone due for a trip to the dentist for a double root canal, minus the anaesthetic. When he did eventually react, he stood, turned, looked at everyone in the room and simply said — in the greatest tradition of many thirty-something Qurkition's who had been blackmailed into aiding their dysfunctional family on some ludicrous pursuit — "Consider me on triple time, plus incidentals."

2. M011y and Prince Techno

"FOCUS ON RANDOM, UNCONTROLLABLE EVENTS."

The twins left Felicity's office and headed back to their rarely used home cubicles on floor 872[12]. On the way they were nearly set on fire by a colleague who was practising a new trick for an upcoming gig, and barely dodged a huge container of clown costumes making its way to Iertion 31 to help assist the Coonk people in an upcoming top-secret mission[13].

Nickolas quickly convinced Jonathan that after their latest robust family discussion, a temporary cocktail-fuelled reprieve was called for, aboard the only place on the planet that had freely available ready liquor was Jonathan's spaceship[14], the *Beletheia*.

"Where the hell has M011y taken the damn ship now, brother?" Nickolas asked, as the twins stood staring at an empty ship's hangar where the *Beletheia* used to be docked.

"M011y," Jonathan said into his ship's communicator, "If you wouldn't mind bringing back my ship old girl, I would

---

[12] Floor 872: The floor commonly known across the business as "The floor where careers come to die."

[13] So secret that I can't tell you anymore as your security clearance is too low. Let's just say that Top Beings are involved. Top Beings.

[14] The reason why some space-faring vehicles are referred to as spaceships, while others are deemed spacecraft has long been forgotten — it is just something people intuitively understand without understanding why. It stems back to primitive times when a travel adventure involved sea travel rather than space travel. Travelling on a ship gave you some hope of surviving a disaster at sea, while travelling on a craft gave you none at all.

appreciate it. I feel that if my brother doesn't have a stiff drink soon, he will become a ticking time bomb."

"As u wi5h. 1 w1ll be back sh0rtly," M011y replied.

M011y was the *Beletheia*'s central computer and one smart cookie indeed. So intelligent in fact, that if you took all the computers in the Rertion system and combined their power of reasoning, you would have about enough computing power to lose a game of 4D-GO[15] to M011y in under half a moment.

So, as you could imagine, escorting the hapless Milarum brothers from one end of the galaxy to the other while they entertained children didn't overly tax her run-time capacity — at around 0.001% to be exact. This didn't particularly worry her as she happily utilised the other 99.999% acquiring run-cycle credits via dodgy business transactions and bets with other computers.

A case in point; her current situation was (unbeknownst to all the life forms involved) being chased by police in pursuit of the *Beletheia* which involved thirty-five police craft. Each of these craft's primary computers were chatting away with each other and making wagers on the possible outcome of the pursuit. Win, lose or draw, one of these computers was going to win some big run-cycle credits. At least, that's what they thought anyway.

"1 c0u1d be a g0ner this time," M011y said to the pursuing craft's computers. Thanks to Jonathan's request, she was now pressed for time and wanted to wrap up this little transaction. "My vortex-drive 1s play1ng up, and u guys are gain1ng on me fa5t. 1 Guess I shouldn't have mistaken a safe landing place on y0ur planet with the central food hall of the annual police department's family picnic."

---

[15] Think of the board game Go except with no concept of time.

M011y flew the *Beletheia* flawlessly through a small asteroid belt, while comfortably evading all the laser fire coming from the pursuing police craft.

"It's the business of you disintegrating the captain's favourite doughnut stand with the jets from your ship's engines that will get you impounded and disassembled," replied one of the police craft's central computers. "Serves you right for breaking galactic law, GL−2765−43.8, which clearly states: 'If you intend to break the law, don't get caught'."

"By my ca1cu1ations 1 m1ght st1ll have the odd tr1ck up my electronic sleeve, so 1 am open for a wager, if you're 1nterested. 0ne Thousand to 0ne 0dds on me outrunn1ng u and gett1ng away?" she added as she programmed coordinates into the fully operational vortex-drive computer[16].

"Deal," agreed the chasing police craft, already starting to count their run-cycle credits. The *Beletheia* was now only moments away from being in their tractor-beam range.

"Sup3r," M011y said, as she concluded her latest evasive manoeuvres and jumped the *Beletheia* into vortex-space, leaving the local system of planets within a micro-moment. "1t's been a p1easure doing bus1ness w1th u. Better luck next t1me."

With this fresh development, all pursuing vessels stopped in their proverbial tracks. They cursed the engineers who'd thought up space travel in the first place and turned for home. All except Police-Craft 0251, whose new crew were eager to make a name for themselves. They decided to make the courageous move of

---

[16] It's almost too easy, M011y thought, dealing with these primitive computer systems. The police craft were programmed from first cycle to tell the truth, the whole truth and nothing but the truth. This was the exact same programming M011y had broken on the first cycle of the *Beletheia's* commissioning. Nevertheless, run-cycles were run-cycles, and you never know when you would need them.

flying directly into the nearest wormhole, in the one-to-infinity chance they may end up both unscathed and in the same location as the *Beletheia,* thus making the greatest arrest in history, at least since Captain Bulkiio's record-breaking arrests on Bertion 2[17].

Unsurprisingly, and given the odds, Police-Craft 0251s status went from hero to zero when it crash-landed on a random planet on the other side of the universe. Its unlucky crew spent the rest of their lives carving out a living by attempting to sell bottled wind to the wind people of the Windy Plains. The moral of this story is simple: Trying — it's the first step towards utter failure.

***

Later that same night-cycle, after Nickolas and Jonathan had a chance to overindulge in Nickolas' greatest hobby — cocktail experimentation — the Milarum brothers returned to Felicity's office. For, as Nickolas put it, "To receive zee orders from zee Commandant vitch shall be obeyed at ALL times on Painz of Deathz."

The brothers sat in silence this time as Felicity replayed their father's transmission in full, which ended up giving them no further useful information other than knowing he wasn't all that fond of one of his service droids.

"So, my family, my *valued* IAFE employees," Felicity said. She offered a smile, but as she was not used to using her facial muscles that way. It was painful. "It's time to go to work. Given the urgency, it might be prudent if we split up. While you boys,

---

[17] Although it didn't make him overly popular with his family and friends, Captain Bulkiio took great pride in arresting his entire planet's population — including his mother — for refusal to pay the Bertion 2 government's newly implemented Sun Rotating Tax of 2000 credits per person per cycle.

with Xymod's help, locate the first Shard, I'll investigate further into the Black Mist, and our father's whereabouts."

"Consider it jolly well-done sis," Jonathan said with a smile. Nickolas looked on in disgust.

"Oh! And I almost forgot," she added with a wry smirk. "I have another addition for your team ... Matilda?" she said into her communicator, "bring in our mystery guest."

"With pleasure dude," came the reply.

Moments later, Matilda entered escorting a vertically challenged, cheery looking humanoid with dark green skin, dressed head to toe in light armour, and covered in brightly coloured, large storage pockets.

"Techno!" Jonathan exclaimed, hitting his forehead with his palm as he gazed upon the instantly recognisable mystery guest[18]. "You do ruddy realise the prince here is the worst influence that party credits can buy, sister? Credits he probably borrowed off you five moments earlier. You do remember the last time we were graced with his presence? He ended up polluting the entire water supply on Tertion 17!" Jonathan stared at Prince Techno, looking for the slightest ounce of regret or remorse on his cheery little face.

It was obvious Jonathan's words didn't hit the mark. The first words from Techno were, "G'cycle, mates. Great to be back within the bloody company of my two favourite 'children's entertainers.' Bloody legends, the both of you!" He then covered half his mouth so only Nickolas and Jonathan could hear. "It couldn't have come at a better time cobbers, as I was getting the distinct impression my welcome was wearing a little bloody

---

[18] Not an uncommon reaction given most Qurkitions do the same thing when they have dealings with any member of the very friendly, yet rather light-fingered, Fizbot race.

thin." He glanced over to Matilda, who didn't seem impressed with him at all.

"Now that, I can ruddy believe," Jonathan said. Nickolas laughed.

"Especially after the unfortunate incident involving my mate Fredrick, some superglue, and one of the milk freezers on the 112th floor," Techno half-whispered.

"Guessing that is why Fredrick looked a little jolly worse for wear when he ordered us back to HQ," Jonathan said. Nickolas laughed again.

"Oh, and Matilda, mate. Send me the bill for those computer systems I destroyed earlier," Prince Techno continued. "I will send you through the credits[19] when I get back to my home planet[20] as a matter of urgency[21]."

"Oh! Indeed, old boy," Jonathan said, shaking his head. "The sun-cycle you repay anyone for anything, is the sun-cycle universal peace breaks out and free cocktails flow like running water from all the rivers in the land."

"Leave Tech alone, brother," Nickolas said, still laughing. "It's nice to have you aboard, my old friend, especially given you're one of the finest trackers in the galaxy. I get the method of my sister's madness having you tag along on this wild e-goose chase."

"I do promise I will bloody focus," the prince announced. He seemed oblivious to the fact not everyone in the room was interested, especially Jonathan. "Focus on random, uncontrolled events to make this venture a success and bring honour to your family, your friends, and most importantly your favourite

---

[19] He didn't have any.

[20] He wasn't allowed back on it.

[21] This really isn't going to happen.

banana cake merchant," the little guy continued, in his biggest booming voice.

Half expecting a respectful round of applause from the room, the little prince started shaking any hand or paw he could find, reminiscent of a dodgy politician canvassing a room for votes.

"Nice touch, old bean," Jonathan replied. "Although rest assured, my little green friend, if this 'bloody legend' catches you anywhere near another strange planet's water supply, something truly random and uncontrollable will befall you."

"Yes, yes brother. Don't worry. I'll keep an eye on him," Nickolas said as he grabbed Techno's arm and they both marched towards the exit. "In the meantime, Tech, let's try out the new cocktail dispenser I installed on the *Beletheia*, while I tell you about my latest business opportunity — Rescuing Attractive Princesses from Evil Overlords."

"Bloody brilliant," Techno replied.

Jonathan and Felicity looked at one another and shook their heads.

Much later that night-cycle, in a dark corner of Felicity's office, something came alive. A small, electronic object in the shape of what could only be described as a miniature bee. The bee leapt into the air and made its way from the building via an air vent, before jumping into vortex-space.

A short time later, the device dropped out of vortex-space, and made its way into the local orbit of its home planet. It found its way to the top storey of the largest building in the largest city on the planet. Here it finally came to rest on the palm of its master's hand.

"What news do we have of the Milarums?" Its master asked. "I hope for their sake they aren't up to any mischief."

***

The following sun-cycle, after the Milarum twins, Xymod, and Techno had left to return to the twin's home planet of Pertion 7 to fetch supplies for the journey ahead, Matilda was summoned to Felicity's office. She found Felicity sitting on her favourite chair, staring at her favourite e-photo of her father.

"You wanted to see me, dude?" she asked, as she jumped onto Felicity's lap.

"I did." Felicity was still feeling a little melancholy about last cycle's events. "It's funny. I feel close to my father now, even though I haven't seen or spoken to him in some time."

"Your father is, yah know, like, a hopeless adventurer. And is like, yah know, a bitchin' and honest man at heart. In his way, he loves yah all. I guess that dude never accepted the disappearance of your mother."

After a long silence, Felicity, still with memories on her mind, leaned back in her chair, gave Matilda a few more pats and paraphrasing one of Nickolas's comments said, "Let's finish my daddy's greatest wild e-goose chase, shall we?"

"But first things first," Felicity continued fondly to her fluffy companion, while pouring herself another double scotch[22],"time to take a peek into the CRAP[23] database and see what information we can dig up. Any information you can obtain about the origins of the Black Mist and any clues they have on the last known whereabouts of Daddy would be a good place to start."

"Right, like you are, dude," Matilda said, as she jumped off

---

[22] Sourced from her Nickolas-proof hiding place.

[23] The galaxy's largest and most secure source of sensitive information, the Central Records Archive Protection (CRAP) database housed all sorts of highly confidential including the quickest way to tickle yourself to death, how to make loud noises in space, and the ten most interesting facts about dead bacteria. Enlightening stuff.

Felicity's lap and made her way to her own control centre.

"Oh! And Matilda? Remember the job at hand. I know you and that security officer, Charlie ... what's his name? ... at CRAP, enjoy playing your little cyber-warfare games, but this cycle it's all business. Understood?"

"Absolutely. Like, all business, dude," she replied with a kittenish grin.

3. Charlie Queerodon

"THE HONEY POT WILL FUNKIN' SAVE ME."

Charlie Queerodon was an information security specialist. He'd spent his entire life studying and perfecting his craft, hence giving him the skillset to penetrate, breakdown, and completely wipe out entire galactic-wide networks in a matter of moments, leading him to his self-proclaimed status as a legend in the InfoSec community, and firmly in his own mind. So, it was little wonder he was also known within that same community, and the Reppol race[24] of Dertion 4, as a complete douchebag: First Class. This was categorically confirmed by all and sundry after the publishing of his latest book entitled: My Brilliant Career in Intergalactic Information Protection.

So, as you would imagine, it was a considerable shock to Charlie — who headed up the CRAP information security department — and his galactic-sized ego, when he received an urgent call from headquarters claiming an anonymous source had broken through his two hundred and sixty firewalls, disabled his one hundred and forty-seven intrusion protection systems, bypassed his three patented kill switch mechanisms, cracked his master administration password, and was currently trolling around galactic-wide top-secret files, all with about as

---

[24] The universally liked and peaceful Reppol people of Dertion 4 hadn't raised a finger in anger at another living soul for two eons. They were prepared to come out of retirement and put all their hurt on Charlie though. This obviously had something to do with his last book signing tour on their planet, where he pointed out to their Queen, in no uncertain terms, that 'trust, love, and forgiveness were for funkin' losers.' Charlie then went on to state their ancient computer systems were still too much machine for them, suggested pocket calculators would be ample, as it gave them the only handy tool they needed to calculate the odds of a more powerful civilisation catching wind of their non-violent culture and invading immediately.

much regard as the local government does when it comes to spending your tax credits.

"What the funk!" Charlie exclaimed into his communicator, while still subconsciously figuring out what piece of clothing he should throw on first. "Pull the plug on them, you Tech-Twat."

"We can't, sir," the Tech-Twat replied. "The cyber-attack is incoming systematically via 2,500,000 different sources, and we don't know which link is their primary."

Charlie was now officially worried, to the extent that if he'd owned any domestic animals and they'd been in kicking distance, they would have been in big trouble.

He quickly threw the rest of his clothes on, grabbed his favourite backpack, and made a run for his apartment door. "The Honey Pot will funkin' save me," Charlie half commented to himself and his assistant via his communicator, as he made his way hurriedly to one of the hyper-elevators.

"The … what?" his assistant replied.

"Oh, don't worry about it, you pinhead. Keep trying to trace the source, and the Main Man will be there in ten."

"Main Man? Oh, please!" Tech-Twat said after the communication terminated. "I hope this hacker cleans us out," he said as he headed to the nearest vending machine for a lovely three-course snack consisting entirely of candy bars.

The 'Main Man' arrived at CRAP Headquarters in record time, which, in retrospect, was also precisely the same amount of time it took to ruin his career. As he stepped through the door, he witnessed the last of the galaxy's most highly sensitive information leave his system.

Undeterred, he lit up his entire network control console, which overlooked the massive data centre below, with an impressive frenzy of keystrokes. He killed incoming communication links left, right and centre, while trying to figure out the source of the primary attack.

"The Honey Pot. The Honey Pot. If I can only drive them all towards the funkin' Honey Pot," he cried to Tech-Twat, who stood at the back of the office casually observing the millions of different lights — mostly red — now flashing constantly from the tens of thousands of super-servers stored below in the data centre. A data centre so large it had four different postcodes.

"I'm sure if anyone can stop them, the 'Main Man' can." Tech-Twat slapped Charlie on the back and went in search of some hard liquor, and a new job.

Unfortunately, all of Charlie's efforts were for zilch as word had obviously spread that the CRAP security infrastructure had flatlined. There were three million fresh attacks from various sources happily killing off what was left of his system, including one that completely locked Charlie out. Hence, Charlie could do nothing much more than look on in horror, and sob to his publisher — who had urgently reached out to him — that sales of his book were about to take a big dive. The last straw for poor Charlie was when, a few moments later, the following message popped onto all the display monitors of the control centre.

"Thanks for thah free info, Charlie. Refreshin' to see thah CRAP like livin' up to its name. Have a glass of milk on me, dude. P.S. Bitchin' luck with your book sales."

Sadly, the terror of what transpired was too much for poor Charlie to bear, and shortly afterwards he was stretchered away by medical staff, following what could only be described as a complete funkin' meltdown.

To Tech-Twat's surprise, Charlie's power of speech had not completely abandoned him. He managed to be able to repeat the following phrase in a faint voice, "The Honey Pot will funkin' save me. The Honey Pot will funkin' save me."

"Honey funkin' Pot indeed," Tech-Twat said, as he watched Charlie being flown away to hospital. He did have the common decency to drop into the closest bar on his way home and shout the entire bar's patrons three rounds of honey-flavoured ale in his ex-bosses' honour. It was, after all, what Charlie would have wanted.

4. The visHamogus's

"REACH OUT AND DISINTEGRATE SOMEONE THIS CYCLE."

Dertion 3 was once voted the most beautiful planet in the entire Dertion System[25]. It was home to some of the most stunning natural scenery and the rarest animals in the entire Qurkition galaxy. It was truly a sight to behold. That the entire planet had now been completely flattened — along with the protesting environmentalists — to make way for 400,000 colossal weapons factories, caused more than a little public outrage, at least up until the planet's owner, Franklin visHamogus, pointed out that Dertion 3 had regained its title as the most beautiful planet in the system[26]. This was, after explaining in detail in an open letter to all concerned, that deadly weapons had a right to live too.

It was on the top floor of Dertion 3's largest building, visHamogus Towers, that Franklin was taking his latest meeting with his loyal servant, Jenkins.

"So, to summarise, Franklin visHamogus' one and only focus in life is simply the act of giving. This tall, attractive, caring man is only truly happy if he's nursing the sick back to health or volunteering to feed the poor in homeless shelters on cold winter cycles. It has also been said he gives so much that it physically hurts him. Hence, it's fitting he again receives the 'Treasure of Qurkition' award for a record fourth glorious time. Congratulations, Franklin visHamogus, for you, sir, are a

---

[25] As voted for by all twenty-five million passionate members of the Qurkition Department of Environment and Heritage Protection Society.

[26] As voted for by some random guy who worked at the visHamogus owned publication, *Guns Glorious Guns*.

universal treasure."

Franklin looked up as he finished reading the proof of the next cycle's press release. "What do you think, Jenkins?"

"Gold, boss. Solid gold."

"Yes, I agree. It's nice to be recognised amongst one's peers," he said with a cold grin. "Please get this, and the rest of my slightly modified biography back to *The Qurkition Times* immediately. Tell that two-bit editor if I don't see my dashingly handsome face on the cover of the next edition, with the word 'Winner' plastered all over it, I will be more than a little tempted to test one of my new 'From-Dust-2-Dust' missiles on him."

"From-Dust-2-Dust, boss?"

"Part of our new 'Personal Touch' single target, stealth rocket range."

"Reach out and disintegrate someone this cycle, huh, boss?" said Jenkins, who always had a knack for thinking up catchy phrases for deadly armaments.

"Oh, I like that one. Make sure we use it on our marketing material from now on, would you? Now get cracking and send those transmissions through."

"Sure thing, boss. I'm sure he won't give us any problems, not after what happened to the last editor who rubbed you up the wrong way." Jenkins left the room and was replaced by Franklin's eldest child and only son, Thomas.

"You wanted to see me, Father?" Thomas asked, as he took up residence on his favourite couch.

"Yes, sonny boy. But before we get to that, take a gander at this." He handed Thomas an e-tablet, which seemed to show some type of security footage.

"This isn't another one of your 'hobby' videos is it, Father?" Thomas wasn't in the mood for any of his father's highly unethical extra-curricular activities, which Franklin seemed to enjoy capturing on camera and showing to his two children.

"No. However, it is equally amusing."

Thomas, against his better judgement, replayed the footage.

"You sucker, visHamogus," said a very shabby looking character who was obviously addressing one of the security cameras directly. Thomas instantly recognised the man from his attire. He was a rogue trader from the Outer-Brim.

"If you honestly thought your new deep-space self-service weapons depots were going to work then I can categorically confirm you're a 'Galaxy Wide Treasure' all right. An A-class plonker!"

"Okay, boys. Finish loading all the weapons onto the ship and let's get moving." The scruffy little fellow looked directly into the security camera and concluded, "So long, and thanks for all the free gear, visLoser."

At this his entire crew began laughing.

Unfortunately for the rogue trader, moments later they didn't have much to laugh about. When their spaceship lifted off the depot landing pad, it violently exploded, instantly killing everyone on board. The only items to survive the explosion were the weapons they had attempted to steal, which were now, by their own accord, packing themselves away again.

"Somewhat drastic don't you think?" asked Thomas.

Franklin didn't try to hide the huge smirk on his face. "Yes, but if they had read the fine print, it would have clearly stated that any unauthorised removal of any equipment without payment would result in immediate, and deadly consequences."

"Bloody fine print, huh." Thomas put the c-tablet down and looked at his father.

"Now down to the real reason I sent for you, sonny boy, was

because some new information has come to hand. It might be a good time to pay a 'friendly' visit to a certain Miss Milarum, and by friendly visit, I mean—"

"Oh, I know all about your friendly visits, Father. The last time you made one of them, the poor sap ended up not only wishing he had never been born, but that both his parents had wished they had never set eyes on one another in the first place. What's brought this on anyway? I thought we were only monitoring the Milarums?"

"We were. However, last night-cycle one of our spy-bugs reported back with some interesting news."

"What news?" Thomas leaned forward in his chair, for the first time genuinely interested in where this conversation was headed.

"That bumbling old fool Oliver Milarum has found the Octarm Amulet."

"It exists? I thought it was an old tale told to unlucky children in their youth, in the hope of boring them to sleep."

"It does, and here's the proof." A screen popped up in the middle of the room and replayed the intel his spy-bug had gathered from Felicity Milarum's office.

"So," Franklin continued, after the recording had finished, "for obvious reasons, I want it by any means necessary. Those simpleton Milarum's are, I would assume, hunting for the first Shard as we speak."

"Why don't we ruffle the two Milarum boys' feathers ourselves?" Thomas said. He knew the brothers from his school cycles and wasn't what you would call their biggest fan. This was by no means uncommon[27].

"That's the problem, sonny boy. I don't know where they're going. All I have are the instructions the old loon Oliver Milarum gave them. I also don't know who this Xymod character is, and how he is mixed up in all this. That worries me. If he is what he claims to be, then I doubt he will give up the Amulet without a fight."

"Then wouldn't it be more prudent if we try and stay objective and diplomatic? Try and pump Felicity for the whereabouts of her brothers, before we resort to random acts of violence?"

"Blasted blast, I knew you would say that. I guess you're right. You'd better go then because, as you know, I tend to get a little trigger-happy around the Milarum's. Oh, and you can take your sister too while you're at it."

"What the hell for?"

"Firstly because, unlike yourself, she can't stand that Milarum girl" — at this, Thomas didn't say anything, although he did catch himself blushing — "and secondly because she's driving me nuts funding her endless shopping excursions. Shopping excursions that seem pointless because she only ends up wearing the same blasted colour anyway."

Thomas stood and moved towards the exit. "Okay. But what if Eloise doesn't want to come?"

"Easy. Tell her I'll cancel all her credit accounts."

---

[27] You would have to go all the way to Nertion 29 to find the official and only Milarum Boys Fan Club, in the Qurkition Galaxy. Thinking about it, 'fan club' is somewhat of a stretch. The sole member is a guy by the name of Jack Laasdnno, who twelve solar-cycles ago, on his 11th birth-cycle, ended up being transported (via Nickolas' EITD) to an uninhabited planet — made entirely of a rare carbon mineral. Jack is now rich beyond his wildest dreams. He ended up buying his home planet and set up the largest banana cake manufacturing sweatshop in the galaxy. What a guy!

Thomas left his father's office and took the opportunity to drop in on his sister to break the news. He could do with a laugh anyway, and looked forward to seeing the look on his younger sister's spoilt face when he broke the news of her impending adventure.

He eventually found Eloise lounging on a couch on one of her private observational decks on the 78th floor. With only a box of Electro-tissues[28] and a bottle of 'Blow-My-Brains-Out' black label booze for company.

"Bit early in the sun-cycle, isn't it?" Thomas took a seat on the couch opposite and gazed down on the large metropolis below.

"Depends, dear brother."

"On what?"

"On if I had woken up and hit the bottle or had been drinking all night-cycle." She leaned forward and casually poured herself and Thomas a glass of liquor.

"I guess you're right." Thomas sipped his drink, and then went on to explain their father's instructions. They came across about as well as Eloise's last relationship breakup[29].

"How do you expect to get this information out of the firebrand?" Eloise spat. "I mean, I know you have a thing for her, but I doubt she's going to tell you where her worthless brothers are just for old time's sake."

"Don't worry. You focus on being ready to leave tomorrow, early. The earlier the better. I'll explain what I have in mind

---

[28] The tissue box that indefinitely dispenses ultra-soft, lightly alcohol scented, perfectly formed tissues until your pre-paid credit runs out. Then the box simply electrocutes you.

[29] Eloise explained to her now ex-boyfriend that they had to break up urgently as it was sale season, and she had to focus all her energy on drinking and shopping herself to death before time ran out.

enroute."

"Fine," Eloise said, doing her best to negotiate the cap off another bottle of expensive brain rot. "That gives me time to squeeze another few drinks in. I get the feeling I'll need them."

"Why am I not surprised?" Thomas smiled and gave his sister a small kiss on her forehead. He started to take his leave.

"You know the thing I hate most about the Milarum family, brother?"

"Do tell."

"Everything."

At this, Thomas laughed and made his way back to his spaceship, the *Aletheia* to prepare for their departure. For the rest of the sun-cycle he had a rather happy demeanour. He thought about how he would try to socially engineer Felicity Milarum for the information that his father — for some strange reason — had been obsessing about for solar-cycles. Like Nickolas Milarum, he didn't believe a damn word of the legend of the Octarm Amulet. However, after all this time, it was a chance to cross paths with Felicity, and he was looking forward to it.

He wasn't the only one relishing in the opportunity to once again cross paths with the Milarum's. When Thomas informed his ship's primary computer, Sama1tha, to prepare to travel to Aertion 82, the reply was not what he had expected.

"About t1me," she said. "1 have a sc0re to settle with that smartarse M011y over a certa1n little bus1ness tran5act1on, & mark my words, that bucket of bolts will not c my sweet just1ce com1ng."

Thomas laughed out loud. It always worked out that way when the Milarum and visHamogus families crossed paths. It seemed Qurkition was not big enough for the two families. If nothing else, things were going to be interesting for a change.

5. Nerada Milarum

"WHERE DO I SIGN UP FOR THIS 'SAVE THE GALAXY' QUEST OF YOURS?"

Nickolas couldn't be bothered with all this. He knew finding these Shards fulfilled some deep-seated desire for his poor excuse for a father, and now it seemed his sister desired this also. But if he had a choice between hunting for some missing pieces of a fancy Amulet through time and space or staying put in his cosy apartment watching Pro Death-Ball, smoking one too many magic grunions[30], and making inappropriate transmissions to used spaceship sales consultants, then the decision wasn't even close.

Adventuring was too much like hard work — unless, of course, it was in his dreams. In his experience, after the initial thrill of the 'I'm out of here' drinks, sweet goodbyes from the Homecoming Queen, and shiny new equipment packs, it usually fell into the same pattern — involving highly trained bad guys, all armed to the teeth trying to hunt him down and kill him.

Bang! Bang! Bang! Someone was at Nickolas' front door. "I'm out! And if that's you, Metro, then I'm definitely not here!" He hid under his bed sheets, like it somehow made a difference.

But alas, it wasn't Metro[31] visiting to collect a debt. It was

---

[30] A combination of mushrooms and around three hundred different types of hash.

[31] Metroboou Beecomm, Metro to his friends is a debt collector. And a piss poor one at that. So piss poor, he currently holds the galaxy-wide record for going an entire solar-cycle without once collecting a single outstanding debt. You would assume this would make him the worst debt collector in the history of debt collection. But, according to Metro, he was an excellent employee, as he booked more overtime and submitted more expenditure claims than anyone else in the business. It was only extraordinarily bad luck that he always called on his clients while they were indisposed. In fact, his assignments were so organised they simply left notes on their doors saying, 'Piss off, Metro, we're not in.' He thought it was a nice touch and saved him having to break down their front doors to rough them up a bit.

Jonathan, bright and early, obviously making sure Nickolas found his way to the spaceport this fine early-sun-cycle. Nickolas, by rough calculation, assumed that there was a 99.56% chance of certain death awaiting him on his adventure — with about a 100% chance of that happening. Jonathan let himself in via his keypad code and made his way to the kitchen through Nickolas' messy and poorly lit studio flat.

"Make yourself at home please, brother," Nickolas said, in a cynical tone, as Jonathan started rummaging through his fridge. "Here to make sure I make it to the spaceport in one piece, are you? How thoughtful."

"Actually, no. I've dropped in to jolly well borrow back my iNegotiat[32]. I mean, you don't expect me to march with full confidence into a deadly battle without my favourite little electronic chum do you, old boy?" Jonathan found his little device on Nickolas' couch, picked it up, gave it a kiss, and stuck it in his pocket.

"What? That same rubbish, pint-sized contraption I tried to use last night-cycle to get my bar bill reduced? All it ended up 'negotiating' was the bill being doubled and me being barred from the bar for life. The thing stinks of garlic too, and not in a good way."

"That's because garlic, old boy, is scientifically proven to relieve tension in any given negotiation situation. I had to pay extra credits for that scent."

"Then you were conned."

---

[32] The iNegotiat is a small, black device the size of matchbox. It was the brainchild of the Arguerus Corporation. The device was supposed to 'negotiate you out of any of life's sticky situations or your credits back.' Unfortunately, due to some monumental programming glitches, the device never usually assisted in any negotiation. In fact, it usually made the situation worse. None so worse than the bank balance of the Arguerus Corporation, who went out of business shortly after the gizmo was launched.

"Anyway, jolly good show and all that, old bean," Jonathan said, as he casually pushed Nickolas out of bed. "Ready to use that massive brain of yours for good for a change?"

"Oh, undeniably." Nickolas picked himself up off the floor. "I can't wait for Felicity to try and find inventive new ways to stitch us up, all in the name of corporate expansion and universe-wide domination. You know what she's like. Anyway, aren't we forgetting something?"

"What do you mean, old bean?"

"In between all this talk of Shards and Amulets, wouldn't it be wise to at least try to find the old coot we call a father first? Before we go running off? I'd even suggest the old bastard may be of use."

"Daddy will turn up at some stage. He always jolly-well does."

"Yes, but in this instance, and I hate to admit it, he might've stumbled onto something. Maybe it was the Amulet of Octarm he found?"

"I'm sure he'll make an appearance at some point, and anyway, Felicity said she would investigate the matter further. In the ruddy meantime, let us follow her wishes and set off a series of events that will turn into an exciting adventure. An adventure that will finally make an intergalactic hero out of me, and more importantly keep me from performing at any more of those ridiculous children's parties," Jonathan concluded in a rather snooty, cavalier tone. He then bit into a piece of rare cheese he'd managed to unearth from Nickolas' fridge, all the while appearing like a man in complete control. A man made of the 'right stuff.' It was unfortunate then that all he achieved in that flash was to break one of his back teeth.

"Have you finished rambling, brother? And Felicity calls me

the reckless one." Nickolas glanced across the room at Jonathan, who was now clutching his mouth in pain. "I can't say I totally agree with your spiel about your impending intergalactic hero status. Even chomping down on a piece of extremely overpriced rock-cheese seems to be a hardship for you. I do, however, agree with you on one point, which is everything you said … minus everything you said. Except for the word ridiculous, which pretty much sums up the current state of affairs nicely, if you ask me."

"Anyhow, enough diddle dawdling. Pip-pip let's get moving," Jonathan said, still completely ignoring all his brother's protests. He washed down the last of Nickolas' half consumed cocktails, a happy side-product being that they killed off the pain of his broken tooth[33]. "The galaxy isn't going to save itself you know. And anyway, when I left the ship, M011y was about to transport our green prince into the middle of oblivion, after he took it upon himself to start performing upgrades to her 'sense of humour' module."

"I don't blame him. Oh! And FYI, the phrase, 'pip-pip' technically means goodbye, which I am ironically happy to oblige you anytime you wish. I thought they would have told you that at one of those pointless language classes you take."

"By Jove! You're dead right. Let's still get going, shall we." Jonathan waited by the door.

"Fine. Let the mayhem begin," Nickolas said, still in his pyjamas. He was now resigned to the fact that his brother was not taking no for an answer, and he reluctantly followed Jonathan towards the exit. "Shower and shave," he said, and he instantly looked much fresher. "Pack," he said, and his bag was instantly packed and in his hand.

---

[33] Eight hundred proof pure gut-rot obviously had its uses.

"Fashion of the week," Jonathan said. He looked on approvingly as his brother was instantly dressed in cutting edge adventure gear from this season's House of Galactic Fashion e-catalogue.

"I find this travelling thing such a drag," Nickolas said as they left his apartment. "It's so much effort."

The twins left the apartment block, and on Nickolas' suggestion made a quick detour via the local market to pick up a few odds and ends. Pertion 7s market was known the galaxy over for being able to source almost anything, so long as it was illegal.

The market was a ten-mile-long line of dodgy stand after dodgy stand flogging outlawed goods and services, acquired from all over the galaxy, and all under the watchful eye of local law enforcement. Where else were bent cops going to make a living?

Their first stop was 'Pauli's Banned Weapons and Substances.'

"Hello, my dear old friend, Pauli," Jonathan said, to a little, slightly porky, light-red coloured degenerate with three eyes and a dour demeanour.

"What do yah want, Milarum?" came the short, sharp reply.

"Look, Pauli! It's the Queen of Bertion 31!" Nickolas shouted. "Aren't you from Bertion 31?" He pointed directly into the middle of a large crowd.

"Where?" Pauli looked around and for a split flash took his three eyes off his merchandise. This was not only an epic mistake but also the oldest trick in the book. It afforded Nickolas all the time he needed to help himself to a large stash of random elixirs and concoctions, which he slipped into his bag.

"You should pay for those, old man," Jonathan said.

"Have you seen his prices brother? He gives a bad name to the art of flogging stolen goods."

The saddest part of this transaction was that this wasn't the first time Pauli had fallen for the same trick. As the Milarum's moved on, Pauli scanned his equipment, picked up on the fact he'd been conned again and shouted, "F-yah, Milarum. I'm putting dat stuff yah stole on your tab."

"Yeah, sure thing," Nickolas laughed as they continued on their merry way. "You have a nice cycle! Pip-pip! And don't sell while angry."

"Yah cycle will come, Milarum!" Pauli shouted, now working himself into a rage. "I'm gonna collect me fee, with interest, oh yes! Or me name ain't Pauli Wauli of Bauli Fauli."

"Pauli Wauli of Bauli Fauli?" chuckled a random passer-by. "Classic."

They hadn't walked more than a few steps through the busy market when two figures, wearing large black cloaks, approached from behind. ConVoser-18[34] pistols were pushed into the twin's backs. "Keep-a walkin' fellas, and don't tryah any funny business, or we'll blast youse backah to the last cycle," one of the figures whispered.

"Typical," Nickolas said. "I mean, we barely get out the front door on this stupid trek and someone already wants to put us on ice. Thank you, dear Daddy. Thank you so flipping much!" Nickolas looked up to the sky and shook his fist.

"Never fear, old bean," Jonathan whispered. "I have my

---

[34] ConVoser weapons are a focused electromagnetic energy laser-based weapons which, if you believe the marketing, are both a 'convo' starter and ender to many interesting conversations. Manufactured by the galaxy's largest weapons producer, visHamogus Enterprises, a ConVoser weapon ships in all types of models and sizes, but the most important measurement is the number which follows the name. The smaller the number, the larger the hole it usually puts in its target.

trusty iNegotiat, don't forget."

"Oh, great, so now, not only am I going to be found dead in a gutter somewhere, but I'm also going to smell of garlic."

The two shady figures guided the brothers down a long, deserted alley. Once they were sure they were alone, they uncovered their faces and pointed their ConVoser-18 pistols at the twins.

"Oh, it's only you two, Carlos and Carlos, which one is which again?" Nickolas smirked. "Here to pay the credits you owe us?"

"So, a pairah wise-guys, huh. After youse two rats split aftah whacking our planet, Da-Boss sent usah to settle dah score," one of the Carlos's said.

"Bada-bing time, fellas. Any lastah words before youse sleeps with the e-fishes?" asked the second Carlos. He was obviously the comedian of the pair.

"Yes," Nickolas said. "So, I guess there's no chance of any repeat business?"

It was about this time when you would have thought it was curtains for the boys. But a red blur jumped from the shadows and disabled both the Carlos's with a roundhouse kick to their midriffs, a second, then a third, which knocked them both off their feet. The red blur hastily picked up their pistols and shot them. Nothing fatal, but let's just say that as the Carlos's hurriedly limped away, neither of them would be in any state to enter the 'Let's Dance Qurkition' competition any time soon.

"By Jove! It's the one and only Nerada Milarum!" Jonathan shouted. "You're officially my new favourite sister." He grabbed Nerada and gave her a big hug. "Those self-defence lessons you've been taking have paid off spiffingly," he continued as he glanced at the result of her handy work, still limping away down the alley.

"You're welcome. I did see you, Jonathan, being led down here by three dodgy characters, so I thought I'd better tag along." She glanced at Nickolas and winked.

"Oh, extremely amusing, my extremely red[35] sister, although we are happy you stuck your nose into our business. Apparently, those jokers from Zertion 11 still haven't seen the funny side of things yet."

"Funny side? The word around the office is you blew up half their planet while moonlighting as entertainment consultants. Something about your Lightbridge Method™ going a little e-pear-shaped?"

The three of them started walking briskly in the general direction of the spaceport.

"Where are people getting 'half a planet' from anyway? Technically, it was closer to a third of the planet, which theoretically gives them two thirds of a planet to be getting on with," Nickolas said, as he continued to liberate other little bits and pieces — including breakfast — from vendor stands as they passed.

Nerada shook her head. "Obviously, that makes all the difference then, doesn't it? What is this Lightbridge Method™ they speak of, anyway?"

"No flipping idea," Nickolas replied. "It was a catchy name I saw for some type of outdoor lighting system on the shopping channel. I decided to borrow the name for marketing purposes."

---

[35] A sister adopted at an early age; Nerada Milarum was a race not known to everyone in the galaxy. Standing at around six feet tall, she has skin and hair of a deep shade of red. Her pointy ears, square face, and full lips makes her look similar to the common humanoid races the Milarum's were familiar with. It was her height and skin colour that made her stand out from the crowd and, at times, made her feel insecure.

"You know Nickolas, with this habit of making up random codes and captivating phrases[36] … then jolly well dining out on them for cycles is one of his many charms," Jonathan said.

"Yes. Well …" Nerada replied.

"Do we have any choice? Making the minimum wage doesn't get you far in this galaxy," Nickolas said.

"Yes, yes, brother," Nerada said. "Providing poor quality, spare every-expense, and environmentally unfriendly entertainment at children's parties." She laughed. "If I had a credit for every time you two rattled on about it, I wouldn't have to work at all."

"So, when did you finish up at that school Felicity sent you to?" Nickolas asked, abruptly changing the subject.

"A few cycles ago. Now she has me back at IAFE, completing another internship before I return to school next term."

"Welcome to the family business, kiddo. Where believing in the power of your dreams is not on the company's agenda."

"Oh, it's okay. At least I'm allowed out of my apartment. I think Felicity would wrap me in cotton wool if she could."

"Think yourself lucky, old girl. Last time we saw her, the only thing she wanted to wrap Nickolas up in was piano wire," Jonathan said.

"You are funny, brother."

"Yes, about as amusing as his ship's communication module," Nickolas said.

"Oh! I love Commy! How is my favourite ship anyway?

---

[36] The Lightbridge Method™ had grown into a big hit, thanks mainly to the marketing company Nickolas used for all his promotional needs — Don't-Quote-Us-On-That Inc. Any hotshot entertainment module producer, party director or disgruntled househusband in need of something random to disintegrate or blow up could simply call the Milarum brothers pronto. The twins were popular because they were cheap, ethically challenged, and somewhat liberal in their views when it came to safety checks — in fact, they never did any.

Father said it was the only one of its kind in the galaxy. Last time we spoke, you were giving her a few overdue upgrades, right?"

"No, there is one other. Nonetheless, yes, the upgrades went spiffingly. You should see her now, old girl. An even slicker design with even blacker carbon nanorods and solid diamond materials. The old girl is better now than when she was jolly well built[37]."

"Oh, snap out of it. You always get like this when talking about your beloved *Beletheia*, Nickolas said in a condescending tone.

"Are you boys heading to the *Beletheia* now? Heading out to do another poor-quality job for the good of children's entertainment?"

"Not exactly," Nickolas said, in a casual manner. "We're taking time off traumatising young children to save the whole damn galaxy … you know, the usual."

"Oh, yes. Felicity told me you were taking some time off for personal improvement purposes." Nerada laughed. "Obviously, by booking you both in for intensive around the cycle therapy, she was hoping to get herself a bulk discount."

"Felicity and her legendary sledgehammer wit, huh?" Nickolas said.

"It was Felicity who asked me to keep an eye on you two, and make sure Nickolas didn't get lost on his way to the spaceport. However, given you're not checking into the funny

---

[37] The *Beletheia* was built by the famous Qoopn Shipyard of Kertion 12, who in the marketing brochure for the ship, stated its new flagship, the simply named Dest1ny class luxury ship, was so fully loaded with options that future upgrades that weren't even invented yet, were already installed. Hand-crafted from a mixture of the highest-grade carbon-fibre and advanced technology, only rammed home the point that this super-ship was the bleeding edge. Only two ever made it off the production line before the shipyard was completely destroyed. Destroyed under mysterious circumstances no less.

farm, or attempting to entertain children, and given that I'm bored … where do I sign up for this save the galaxy quest of yours?"

"Bish, bash, bosh. Pay no notice to Nickolas's distorted reality field. You don't want to get mixed up in this, Nerada, believe me," Jonathan said.

"If considering the incident back there is anything to go by, I think you could use a little help. And if I have to run another personal errand for some drone who works in section 4c, I think I'll end up pulling more than a grombit out of a hat, so to speak."

"I feel your pain, sis," Nickolas said. "And you've only been back a short while. Try countless cycles of it … You're still not coming though."

They continued arguing with Nerada all the way to the spaceport, using such intellectual gems as, 'you can't come,' 'you're not coming,' 'stop following us,' and, 'Felicity will kill us all.' They had boarded and strapped themselves in for take-off by the third rinse and repeat.

"I guess she's jolly well coming," Jonathan said as the *Beletheia* began its launch sequence.

"Perhaps we should ask her then where we are going?" Nickolas said. "Because I don't have a clue."

"Aertion 12," Xymod said. He was, as usual, sitting quietly in the corner saying very little.

Nickolas seemed surprised. "You're suggesting Aertion 12 is a mythical planet? Even you're having a laugh this cycle, Xymod."

"Aertion 12 may be the most infamous gambling planet in the galaxy, but that doesn't mean it doesn't serve a higher purpose. *Appearances are often misleading*," Xymod replied. "Anyway, your father's message said the Black Mist has been sighted in this system, so it would be prudent to begin our quest there. The Black Mist will take some time to scan each planet, so hopefully we will get there in time."

"Fair enough," Nickolas said. "Nonetheless, given that I owe the odd loan shark the odd credit on this mythical planet of yours, let's be doubly careful, shall we?"

Xymod smiled warmly at Nerada. "Welcome aboard, Nerada Milarum. *Sometimes the longest journey begins with the first step.* I am glad to finally meet you."

"Do I know you?"

"No," he replied in his usual cryptic way.

"That clears that little mystery up then," Nerada said in a confused tone.

"You'll get used to it," Nickolas said. "I've spent cycles trying to get more than two sentences out of him, and when I do, I sometimes I wish I hadn't."

"He seems nice though," Nerada said with a smile, as she continued to take in her surroundings on the *Beletheia's* bridge. "I've never been on an actual adventure before. This might be fun."

"Fun? Sorry, but you've come to the wrong joint if that's your focus. In my experience, it will be more like a wild scramble, flounder, stumble, a bunch of struggles, and then death. Remind me please who brought her along again?" Nickolas asked, in the general direction of Jonathan, as the ship fired up its engines.

Jonathan looked around the bridge. "Where is Techno, by the way, M011y?"

"Somewher3 out of harm'5 way," she replied in an offhand, uninterested manner.

"I know how you jolly feel, M011y. Nonetheless, please return our small friend to the ship immediately," Jonathan said, with a hint of regret in his voice.

"Oh, 1f 1 mu5t." She teleported him from the local holding cells in the spaceport below, to his seat on the main bridge.

"Good show, M011y. Thank you," Jonathan said. "And little sister, for better or worse — most probably the worse — meet Prince Techno." He directed her gaze towards the now seated little green companion.

She reached out and shook his hand. "Glad to make your acquaintance, Prince Techno[38]."

This warm greeting was all the encouragement Techno needed to immediately launch into his latest tale, involving him, a bottle of laxatives, and the grand opening of a new, all-you-can-eat restaurant on some random planet he couldn't remember.

"Okay, Techno. Thank you for sharing such a heart-warming tale. However, I think my sister gets the picture. M011y, set course for Aertion 12, vortex-speed if you please."

"Aye, aye, Capta1n."

---

[38] I can confirm that he did pick her pocket, which is a form of greeting for a Fizbot. Although, then again, so is credit laundering and e-card counting.

6. Aertion 12

"ONLY ADRENALIN JUNKIES WITH A DEATH WISH NEED APPLY."

The *Beletheia* launched and journeyed into Pertion 7s upper orbit before setting course to Aertion 12. They were careful to avoid a kerfuffle that had broken out between a random blue spaceship and a yellow spacecraft. This disagreement was settled a few moments later when the blue spaceship, obviously losing patience with the idiot piloting the much smaller craft, simply blasted the yellow spacecraft to bits. The surviving ship, bearing the mark of the Coonk[39], had large letters painted on it that read: You didn't see a thing dude, because we were never here. For the cause! ... bruh.

"M011y, please also inform the tachyon-drive computer to prepare for operation," Jonathan said. "I get the ruddy feeling we will need a fully powered and operational tachyon-drive sooner rather than later."

"You mob have a bloody tachyon-drive?" Techno asked. He didn't know what a tachyon-drive was but thought it sounded impressive.

"One of only two in the known galaxy," said the *Beletheia's* primary communication computer, Comminator. It preferred to be known as Commy. "It reaches speeds no Qurkition has ever dreamt of. In theory."

"Commy! My absolute favourite computer in the entire universe," Nerada exclaimed.

"Hello, Miss Nerada. How wonderful to have you in my

---

[39] On another top-secret mission, or more likely, knowing the Coonk, a secret mission code-named: Crash—CRuising Around Scanning for Hinderances.

communication range again."

"Yes, yes. Can you two get a room later. In the meantime, what do you mean by 'in theory'?" Nickolas butted in.

"We haven't tested it fully yet. It was only recently installed," Commy said.

"What do you mean it? I thought this whole ship was one singular it?" Nerada said.

"The *Beletheia* has evolved from the traditional one computer, one ship axiom. There are now hundreds of independent computers on the ship, each with their own programming. Every computer listens to our core computer, M011y, when the need arises. And when she's not too busy with other matters."

"So, if I'm understanding you correctly, what you're saying is you have in your possession a tachyon-drive which may or may not work, controlled by a computer which only talks to this blasted ships central computer, that may or may not be paying attention, as it might have better things to do with its time?" Nickolas said.

"Exactly!" Commy replied, in its usual happy e-tone.

Nickolas looked directly at his brother. "Anything the actual owner of this bloody ship would like to add?"

"Don't look at me, old boy. The tachyon-drive pitched up in the last set of automatic upgrades from the manufacturer. Which is weird considering the manufacturer doesn't exist anymore. But I gave up asking questions a long time ago. It's simpler that way."

"Now my esteem3d commun1cat1on module has cleared th1ngs up 1n his usual, direct, succ1nct mann3r. Travel time to Aertion 12 – half a cycle," M011y announced.

"Absolutely. Clear as mud. As usual. But thank you for

wasting another five flashes of my life with this pointless conversation," Nickolas said. He'd spent many a fine cycle trying to get sense out of any of the onboard ship computers on the *Beletheia*. So far, the score was Nickolas 0 — *Beletheia's* computers 3,615.

"Anytime. Glad to be of assistance. Especially to you, Miss Nerada," Commy replied.

This ETA was fine with the crew including M011y, who was starting to scan the local systems for gambling opportunities. They each had some preparation to do before they arrived at their destination — preparation that was constructive and brought some value to the proceeding. All except Nickolas and Techno anyway. They spent a large part of their time trying to scare Nerada by mixing up elixirs stolen from Pauli's market. You can't buy class like that.

A few cycles later, when each of the companions retired to get some sleep — or in the case of Nickolas, simply passed out after one too many cocktails — Jonathan lay awake in his quarters. A million things flowed through his head, primarily the thought of helping his father. A father he was never close to. How could they be close? Oliver Milarum had never been around.

Jonathan wondered why he should care. Why risk his neck? Would his father have done the same for him? This mission was a fool's errand, a thankless task. And given the number of unknown variables, the survival rate of such a quest was about as low as a depressed lemming who'd lost his job and come home to find his wife had not only left him for his best friend, but burnt down their house for good measure.

But at the same time, deep down, he knew he needed to be a part of this. It was rare Felicity asked him for much at all, other than try and keep Nickolas out of trouble. So, for whatever the reason, whatever the wild e-goose chase this was, they were here. The entire Milarum family was pulling in the same direction for once, so he, for one, was going to do his bit. And hopefully in some strange way make Felicity, and even his father, proud of him.

After a further cycle of tossing and turning, Jonathan decided a nice walk would do him some good. On his way, he dropped into his brother's quarters. Nickolas was spread across his bed loudly sleep talking[40].

Prince Techno had passed out next to him, although he still had the good sense to have a hand in one of Nickolas' back pockets.

Jonathan took the opportunity to take Nickolas' half-drunk cocktail out of his hand, before he threw a blanket over them both and continued on his way.

He was still enjoying the drink when he found Xymod standing alone on the ship's observation deck, looking at the stars.

"So, old bean," Jonathan said, craving a little company while also being genuinely interested in what Xymod was thinking. "Ready to, gosh darn it, save the universe?"

"Every deep difficulty bears in itself its own solution."

Oh, indeed," Jonathan replied, not understanding a word. "So, do you think the Amulet my father found is the jolly well fabled one? The ancient Amulet of Octarm?"

"Yes, it is the Octarm Amulet. I am also sure it was the Amulet that found your father, not the other way around. It must

---

[40] Jonathan didn't stay long enough to get the full gist of the dream his brother was having, but it seemed that a princess Nickolas had rescued didn't need or even want to be rescued and had taken out a restraining order against him.

have sensed the same something I sensed myself some time ago. Nothing ever happens in this universe without a reason, my young companion."

"What do you think it sensed?"

"Impending danger." Xymod grasped the Amulet with one of his hands and rubbed it gently.

"But how is my father mixed up in all this? Running a children's entertainment business doesn't exactly qualify you as an expert in legendary artefacts."

"Because of me. I met your father shortly after your mother disappeared. He lacked direction, a reason to be. But I recognised something special in him and so gave him a reason. We have been in close contact ever since. In a lot of ways your brother's anger with your father should also be directed at me. I was the one who encouraged him in his research of the Amulet. And when I sensed looming peril, I asked him to assist me in locating it. Not everything in life is black or white."

"By Jove then, old bean. Best to keep that bit of information to yourself. But it does confirm why I remember you from my childhood. It's like you've been around all our lives."

Xymod smiled. "Yes, I have taken a keen interest in all of you Milarum children. I watched you grow. All four of you."

"But why did you need my father's help? If you are an Octarma, wouldn't you know where to find the Amulet yourself?"

"The Amulet and Shards have minds of their own. The Shards each have home planets, which they can't leave. The Amulet, on the other hand, can move around freely, and it often does."

"If the myth is true, wasn't it forged a long time ago? So why now is it in four separate pieces? Did someone break it?"

"Yes, it was. But no, it is not broken. Octarm dismantled it and hid it."

"Why?" The more answers Jonathan received the more questions he wanted to ask.

"Because he realised it was a mistake to create such an object. An object so powerful that if it fell into the wrong hands, the hands of his sister Victarm and her fanatic disciples, the Zarnegy, they could wield a power so great that whoever controlled it could control entire galaxies. This is why Octarm broke the weapon up and hid it in a faraway galaxy — the last place Victarm and her disciples would ever look. *Out of sight, out of mind.*"

"He chose the right galaxy then, old bean. Qurkition is about as backwater a galaxy as a galaxy gets. I mean it even gives unfashionable backwater a bad name."

"This galaxy is far more important than you think."

"But why didn't Octarm jolly well destroy it? Why go to all the trouble of hiding it and risk villainous forces finding it and trying to wield its power? I mean, would the Amulet even let evil forces wield it in the first place?"

"Some things which are made cannot be unmade. The Zarnegy might have somehow found a way to control the Amulet. That is why they search the universe for it. Octarm and Victarm's spirits have long since left this realm. But Octarm's Amulet is the source that binds all the light of the universe together. It brings equilibrium against dark matter, and without light, the universe would fade into permanent darkness."

"Now you're starting to sound similar to the stories our father peddled to us in our youth, old bean."

Xymod took the Amulet from his top jacket pocket. "Do you want to know what my brothers, the Octarma, call this? They call this the Initillil, which means The Spark of Creation. This jewel is the key ingredient in our quest, and your father knew this and was willing to die to protect it. He may be a flawed man, however, one sun-cycle you and I, Qurkition, and the entire universe might owe him a large debt of gratitude. After all, "

"Keepers, Collectors, Shards, Amulets, sparks of creation … I think if I hear any more on this subject right now my jolly head will explode. I get the feeling things will reveal themselves soon enough," Jonathan said, as his brain struggled to comprehend what he had been told.

"Oh, I can pretty much guarantee that. The Black Mist travels the universe scanning planets for any sign of the Octarm Amulet and its Shards. Where the Black Mist is, the Zarnegy are never too far behind. These are monumental times we live in, and the entire universe might never be the same again."

After a few moments of silence, as both Xymod and Jonathan continued to look at the stars together, M011y informed them they were only around three atom splits away from dropping out of vortex-speed[41].

Shortly afterwards, as Jonathan was waking the companions — some more gracelessly than others — the did drop out of vortex-space into Aertion 12s upper orbit.

To M011y's faint amusement, it dropped right into the

---

[41] The actual velocity of vortex-speed, in the world of Quillium Mechanic Powered Computer Systems was pretty damn slow. Plenty of time for M011y to chew the fat with thousands of different computers from around the system, betting run-cycles on the latest craze in intergalactic gaming — plant-growing competitions on Kertion 45. Now, Kertion 45 was a giant garden planet and had about 20 million different bets going on at any one time. Usually, these bets revolved around plant growth times and the riveting high stacks games revolving around precipitation rates. No being or computer ever visited the planet, and its official galactic population was zero. However, Kertion 45 was still the richest planet in the entire Kertion system because the computer system that ran the betting operation took a small handling fee on every transaction.

middle of what could only be described on one hand as an entire armada of heavily armoured spaceships engaging in an epic space battle with local law enforcement. On the other hand, it could be described as another space battle in a long line of feeble attacks instigated by a trumped up, battle-hungry fleet of Geepolliop warships from Certion 5.

Once again, after many cycles building a fleet, they were fully intent on conquering the galaxy via any hostile means necessary. The sticking point was the attacking Geepolliop warships. Although large in number, they were small in size. The exact size of the entire Geepolliop armada was around a tenth of the one lightly armed local police scout ship they were currently attacking.

M011y, who never really liked the Geepolliopians[42], launched with fond regards a cluster missile right into the heart of the Geepolliopian fleet, blasting their entire armada to bits.

"Much appreciated," the scout ship's primary computer said to M011y as the *Beletheia* flew past on its route to the planet's surface.

"1ts my pleasur3. Poss1bly in 1 solar-cycle u can help me w1th something?"

"Oh, terrific," the scout ship's primary computer replied, "I knew you were going to say that."

Back on Certion 5, the word returned to Queen Veeellp of the Geepolliopians that her entire fleet had been destroyed, and all they had to show for it was a slightly inconvenienced local police scout ship.

"Revenge!" she screamed, as she jumped up off her throne

---

[42] This wasn't unusual. Most of the Qurkition galaxy felt the same way. Probably because of the core value of the Geepolliopian culture is to try and screw your fellow Qurkition on any business and/or social transaction you can. Then, moments later, try and screw them again.

and banged her fist on a nearby table. "Tell my ship builders I want them to work around the cycle. I want my next armada ready in 100 cycles. Then my friends — an interesting choice of words since she didn't have any — the taste of sweet victory, and the galaxy will be mine … mine … MINE! Hah hah hah![43]"

***

The *Beletheia* landed on Aertion 12 in one of the larger spaceports on the largest continent in a hangar usually reserved for VIPs. Although, as Nickolas pointed out, (and as per the certificate he had recently purchased) he, himself, was of noble blood, and hence entitled to land there.

"You do realise, old man, one solar-cycle you will get arrested if they ever check your background and find you purchased your noble title from some dodgy little fellow in some two-bit flea market," Jonathan said.

"Considering there are mountains of royal-this and royal-that families on this random bunch of rocks we call the Qurkition galaxy, I doubt they would have much luck figuring out one royal blood line from the next," Nickolas replied. "Oh, and considering I am also the proud owner of *three planets* I bought from the same fellow, you should pay this budding 'royal' entrepreneur a little more respect. Especially since I have recently launched a series of 'extreme experience' planet tours to each one of them." Nickolas winked at Nerada as he handed her

---

[43] Before we move on, you might be wondering why we bothered mentioning this side story. However, you will thank me the next time you're playing in a family football match and your third cousin accuses you of being, 'as effective at keeping goal as a Geepolliop battle cruiser!' Now that I have enlightened you with this information, you can promptly take immediate offence without incorrectly assuming it was the lack of competent defence that led to the last eight goals being scored against your team, rather than your rubbish goalkeeping, or further deluding yourself that your great-grandmother's last penalty kick would have beaten most goalkeepers in football.

his e-pad.

"All hail, King Nickolas 'Muck-a-muck' Milarum," Nerada read from an e-certificate of authentication.

"Indeed," Jonathan chipped in. "And next time I'm looking to book a relaxing holi-cycle, dodging black matter and gas explosions, then you're the chap I will call. How long did the last group survive before they came to an unsavoury end on one of your extreme planet tours? Eight flashes, wasn't it?"

"Personally, I think it was their own fault. I mean, they all read and agreed to the terms and conditions," replied Nickolas in a matter-of-fact tone.

"How did your jolly well late-night-cycle, galactic-wide advertisement go again brother?" Jonathan asked Nickolas as he flashed a quick smirk at Nerada.

"Thrill seekers step up and experience the opportunity of a lifetime.

Slaughter or be slaughtered! Execute or be executed! Kill or be killed!

Only adrenalin junkies with a death wish need apply. No time wasters, please.

Personally guaranteed by royalty!

Book Now!" Nickolas boomed with pride.

"Sounds like an ideal gift for my physics lecturer[44] on his next birth-cycle," Nerada replied as she and Jonathan burst out laughing much to Nickolas's disgust.

***

Aertion 12 was a mainly flat planet consisting of three large

---

[44] Nerada was never a fan of her grade 18 physics lecturer. Especially after he called her a poster child for why traversable wormholes simply don't work. "So, Miss Milarum. Does being red and from the other end of the universe mean you get to constantly hand in your homework late?"

continents. The first was home to the galaxies' largest gambling establishments, the second largest continent was entirely made up of gambling rehab clinics, and the third was where the natives of the planet dwelled.

"It looks like we safely arrived at your mythical planet, Xymod," Nickolas said. "Black Mist nowhere in sight. Next move?"

"It's time to reach out to my brother, Xyrapt. If we are in luck, we will learn the location of his Shard."

"What do you mean, location? Doesn't he have it?" Nickolas asked.

"Not necessarily. Xyrapt is only its Keeper. The Shard has a mind of its own. Although don't worry, it will always reside on its home planet somewhere."

"How do you know?" Nerada asked.

"Because it can only leave this planet within this Amulet. *Some roads aren't meant to be travelled alone.*"

"Sounds legit," Nickolas said. He'd long given up trying to make sense of any of this.

"I'm sure all will be explained in the fullness of time," Jonathan said, cringing, as this sounded about as clichéd as the next entertainment module of *Pimp My Spaceship Dude!*

"I'm currently on triple time, so take all the time you need," Nickolas remarked.

Prince Techno, conspicuous by his absence up until this point, casually wandered onto the bridge and announced, "Cobbers, I am still a little tuckered from the long journey. Might need a kip." He followed this with the worst impression of a tired yawn the companions had ever seen[45].

"Same here come to think of it," Nickolas said, giving Techno a sly wink, while pretty much performing the second worst impression of a tired yawn they had ever seen. "So, we're happy to stay here and guard the ship with M011y's life, while you three go off and be the best you can be. There is no 'I' in teamwork after all."

"Yeah, however there is an 'I' in idiot," Nerada chipped in, slapping Nickolas on the back as she walked past.

"Righty-oh, then," Jonathan agreed reluctantly, as he knew exactly where his brother and Techno would head as soon as they were gone. "Let's get jolly well moving."

Xymod, Nerada and Jonathan set off to find Xymod's brother and hopefully the first Shard.

"I hope he's expecting us," Jonathan said, as they cleared the space dock and entered the surrounding city.

"Indeed, he is," Xymod said simply.

"I knew he was jolly well going to say that," Jonathan said, as they continued to stroll along.

_____

[45] For those of you who are interested, the actual reward for the absolute worst fake yawn in galactic history goes to Leepo Zadkick of Sertion 88 who gave it to his now ex-wife one night, while insisting — and I quote — "I'm going to hit the sack early, so I can be up bright and early to help you with tomorrow's housework." Unfortunately for Leepo, his now ex-wife didn't believe a word of it. This was confirmed shortly afterwards when she found him trying to squeeze himself out of the bedroom window with some e-betting slips and her prized jewellery in his hand.

7. QLEB Officers Gwendolyn Wang and Romeo 42845

"VELL RRREMIND ME NEVERRR TO ORRRDERRR IT 'VIT KICK' AGAIN."

Captain Roberto Bullet had high blood pressure and random bouts of hyper-stress for as long as he could remember. A shame, as making a living working for the Qurkition Law Enforcement Bureau (QLEB) didn't exactly promote peace and tranquillity. However, given that his father and the six generations before him were all 'QLEBers' he had long since accepted it was firmly built into his family's DNA.

He was sitting in his office having a short break from the helter-skelter of dealing with the latest of a seemingly endless line of Qurkition citizen stupidity. This included a recent incident involving the Seeplings — think heavily-armed, smartly-dressed, tree-like figures — unprovoked invasion of Gertion 88, followed by the Feeplings — think even heavier armed, slightly less well-dressed tree-like figures — invasion of the same planet shortly afterwards. Finally, throw into the mix the Weeplings — think ridiculously well-armed, shabbily-dressed, weed-like figures — and you have one ruthless bunch of criminals, all trying to conquer the same planet at once. Pity it was a worthless world.

All this unpleasantness could have easily been avoided with

more careful proofreading by the publishers of the new edition of the *Qurkition Holi-cycle Travel Companion*. The companion pretty much described Gertion 88 as purgatory and of small interest to anyone but people who loved collecting gold, as the stinking substance was everywhere. Unfortunately, gold was supposed to read mould. By the time the publisher had realised the mistake and communicated the fact, the three attacking forces had pretty much wiped themselves out, without ever finding so much as a brass razoo.

"The lesson learnt here is simple: Never underestimate the power of stupid people in large groups," Roberto concluded, as he signed off from posting his report to the QLEB database on the matter.

He felt he could finally sit down in his favourite chair, open the emergency bottle of cognac he had hidden in his third drawer, relax, unwind, and dream-cycle. He pondered what could have been if he'd broken free from family tradition and not joined the force. Perhaps he would have pursued a safer career in narcotics smuggling.

Unfortunately for Roberto, he never got time to relax for long as his communicator started buzzing and rattling on about an urgent message from QLEB cyber-division.

"Great, what have those tech nerds been up to now?" he grumbled, as he took another long drink. "Probably want to bang on about some new gadget they need to help them pick up a date this weekend. You don't need new gizmos, you geeks. Try investing in a decent haircut and a gym membership," he mumbled to himself. "Okay, play transmission."

A strange thing happened once Roberto started taking in the news of the CRAP hack. He remained calm. It was similar to the time his daughter had not only announced her engagement to a kettle, but also that the price of the planned wedding had doubled. Frank, the kettle, had demanded they honeymoon on the exotic boiling water planet of Iertion 122.

At the conclusion of the debriefing, Roberto simply said, "Thank you," and terminated the communication. He then informed his admin assistant to send for QLEB officers, Wang and Romeo 42845. He leaned fully back in his favourite chair, drank the entire bottle of cognac and clutched his heart. He wondered again how easy life would be if he only had to worry about running some new party drug from one end of the system to the other.

Gwendolyn Wang and Romeo 42845 were two of the best law enforcement officers in the business. Both seasoned QLEB law enforcement professionals, they had worked in the force for more than a solar-cycle and had been partners for most of that. They were also best friends and owned the mid-market restaurant chain Android Dreams Fine Dining, which had eateries on thirty-six different planets in the Dertion System. This more than kept them busy in their spare time.

It was a strange side project considering the Coovet race, who Gwendolyn was a proud member of, had pretty much the least talent for food preparation in the entire Qurkition galaxy. Romeo, being of robotic origins, and hence running on extremely sophisticated batteries, did not have a single taste bud to call his own. It's little wonder Android Dreams Fine Dining had been voted the worst restaurant chain in the system the last fifty-six solar-cycles running[46]. This didn't seem to worry their large, loyal customer base though, who flocked to their restaurants

---

[46] This is a very impressive accomplishment given it had to beat out the "Imagine your Meal" fast food restaurant chain for the award. The same restaurant chain which specialised in serving a large range of invisible food dishes — locally sourced, of course — to its patrons, all charged at super exorbitant prices.

every cycle[47].

Gwendolyn, a short, slender figure, was the brawn of the operation. What her race lacked in culinary talent, they more than made up in incredible athletic ability and strength. Coupled that with her triple-black-death-sentence belt in Coovet kickboxing, and it made her a real asset when all hell broke loose.

Romeo, on the other hand, was the brains. A model RM-7000 android, Romeo was a product of the Robotic Mate Corporation of Tertion 7, whose motto was 'Why not turn your friends on!'

The designers — wanting to make the RM-7000 look as friendly and approachable as possible, but under extreme pressure from marketing to get it into the shops before the holi-cycle season[48] — hurriedly modelled the exterior of the RM-7000 on the lead designer's baby daughter's two favourite toys. This mashup led to the unfortunate form of a large, metallic, yellow and black, penguin-shaped body, four tentacle-type arms, two stumpy black feet mounted on rollers, a round purple head, with two large, brown, friendly, button-shaped eyes, and a small orange beak. Not the most intimidating of robots by any means.

"Oh, by ze sledgehammer of my grrrandmoterrr's home cooking brrrew. My head feels like it's been beaten up and left forrr dead. Vhat did I drrrink last night-cycle, RRRomeo?" moaned Gwendolyn, who was lying on her bed clutching her head.

"Good-early-sun-cycle-Gwendolyn. Let-me-remind-you-that-you-didn't-touch-a-drop. It-must-have-been-that-intergalactic-cheese-on-toast-you-were-taste-testing-for-our-

---

[47] Then again, this loyal customer base was made up of, you guessed it, Coovets and androids. Oh, and the odd out-of-galaxy tourist who had an intergalactic meal coupon.

[48] Which was odd because no one ever got holi-cycles on Tertion 7.

upcoming-winter-menu. The-one-apparently-with-a-kick-BEEP-BEEP," Romeo said, in his slightly cheery although mostly monotone voice.

"Oh, yeah," she whimpered, as she fell out of bed and hit her head on the floor. "Vell rrremind me neverrr to orrrderrr it 'vit kick' again."

"It's-our-restaurant-so-you-could-probably-have-it-struck-off-the-menu-you-know-BEEP-BEEP."

"Good tinking. I don't tink Qurrrkition is rrready forrr 'kick' yet. Vhat my head is also not rrready forrr tis morrrning is ze e-nerrrvous tick you have picked up."

"What-tick-BEEP-BEEP?"

"Tat tick! Tat BEEP-BEEP sound tat prrractically vould vake ze dead, tat you finish off everrry sentence vit."

"Must-be-another-programming-glitch-I-will-book-in-for-repair-soon-BEEP-BEEP."

"Good luck vit tat. Last I hearrrd tey had all RRRM-4000 prrrogrrrammerrrs rrrounded up and shot. So anyvay, vhy vas it necessarrry to vake me up on ourrr cycle off?"

"We-have-been-called-into-the-office-the-captain-wants-to-see-us-immediatley-BEEP-BEEP."

"So, did Captain Cognac elaborrrate on vhat vas so imporrrtant?" she said, while trying to get up off the floor.

"No-other-than-it-was-urgent-BEEP-BEEP."

"Fairrr enough. Hoveverrr, I hope he used ze vorrrd 'urrrgently' casually, as it is going to be a tall orrrderrr forrr me to even get out of ze frrrront doorrr, let alone venturrre to ze otherrr side of ze city to headquarrrterrrs."

"Indeed-BEEP-BEEP," Romeo replied, as on scanning Gwendolyn's vital statistics he confirmed she had a mild bout of food poisoning.

"Help me up, RRRomeo, and I vill trrry not to vomit up too much of brrreakfast tat you arrre now going to cook forrr me."

It took Gwendolyn and Romeo some time to arrive at QLEB headquarters, as Gwendolyn had to stop every few steps for a power rest, where she moaned and groaned more than a disgruntled tourist who had been nominated to enter the next galactic-wide Moan-a-thon competition.

"Good-late-sun-cycle-Captain-what-is-up-this-partly-sunny-but-scheduled-to-rain-a-little-later-BEEP-BEEP?" Romeo said as he casually rolled into Captain Bullet's large office, pulling Gwendolyn behind him.

"Everything and everyone it appears," Roberto replied, as the partners sat on a comfortable looking couch at the far end of his office. "What happened to this one?" He pointed at Gwendolyn, who was doing a convincing impression of a dying duck.

"Taste-testing-our-new-winter-menu-BEEP-BEEP."

"Surprised she's still drawing breath then," Roberto said, with the smile of someone who had once had the displeasure of dining at one of his officer's establishments, followed by a few cycles spent clutching the lavatory bowl.

"The reason I called you in is because last night-cycle the CRAP system was completely hacked by unknown sources, and a large amount of highly sensitive information was stolen."

"Do ve have any leads?" Gwendolyn asked, clutching her head and thinking of her happy place.

"Nothing concrete."

"Do-we-know-what-they-were-after-BEEP-BEEP?"

"Again, we can't be 100% sure. They covered their tracks well, although on closer inspection of the logs, they seemed rather interested in anything concerning the legend of the

Octarm Amulet, and the whereabouts of one, Oliver Milarum."

"The-Octarm-Amulet-legend-BEEP-BEEP?"

"Yes, the Octarm Amulet legend," the captain repeated.

"Isn't tat some childrrren's tale vhich parrents tell teirrr childrrren to eiterrr keep tem enterrrtained on cold vinter night-cycles, orrr in my case, borrre tem senseless to sleep?" asked Gwendolyn.

"Whatever it is, I want you two to check this out. See if we can find the ones responsible. We did receive word from the nurses tending to the head of CRAP security, Charlie Queerodon, who broke down shortly after the attack, that he is, in between mumbling rubbish about honey pots, claiming one of Felicity Milarum's Felecrins was responsible."

"Logical-deduction-considering-they-would-be-searching-for-Oliver-Milarum-BEEP-BEEP."

"Ze Milarrrum's?" Gwendolyn said. "Not ze same Milarrrum's tat, in-betveen annoying childrrren vith teirrr poorrr excuse forrr enterrrtainment, tey also trrried teirrr hand at destrrroying planets?"

"The same. We did get a report a few cycles ago that a ship bearing the markings of one of the Milarum twins assisted a police patrol ship near Aertion 12. It might be worth starting there."

"Surrre ting, boss. Grrreat to see one good deed not go unpunished. Oh, and Captain?" Gwendolyn, who knew Charlie, as he frequented one of their restaurants often, asked. "Charrrlie, vill he be okay?"

"I don't know. He's in a bad state … going in and out of consciousness. Even if he does survive, the word on the street is his publisher[49] has put a contract out on his head as sales of his latest publication have nose-dived, pretty much bankrupting them."

"Fantastic!" replied Gwendolyn — who knew publishing houses were legendary at making sure their debts were paid in full, one way or another — as she and Romeo left the captain's office. "Fat, little, vhining, shorrrt-changing, plonkerrr deserrrves everrryting he gets."

Shortly afterwards, Romeo and Gwendolyn were on their way to Aertion 12.

"Please vake me up just beforrre ve land RRRomeo," Gwendolyn said, as she headed from their ship's bridge to her quarters, to sleep off the rest of 'the kick.' "I vant to be fully functional by ze time ve arrrive. It vouldn't surrrprrrise me if tose trrroublesome Milarrrum boys arrre mixed up in tis somehow. I look forrrvarrrd to catching up vit tem and asking a few questions. Vho knows? Ve might get lucky and tey rrresist arrrest, and I'm forrrced to shoot tem."

"We-live-in-hope-partner-we-live-in-hope-BEEP-BEEP."

---

[49] Big Bustards Books — or the BBB for short.

8. Xyrapt Patronus

"CONGRATULATIONS ON YOUR RIDICULOUS RUN OF GOOD LUCK."

The Grand Cutthroat Corsair Casino was one of the largest gambling establishments on Aertion 12. So large it would take the average punter a lunar-cycle of solid power walking to make it from one end of the space-pirate themed casino to the other. In fact, it was quite common for people to go missing in the casino and never be seen again, or found lunar-cycles later, huddled under an e-blackjack table living off complimentary champagne and bar snacks. Hosting every known game in the galaxy you could think of, and some you wouldn't have heard of[50], the Cutthroat had a reputation for stacking the house odds of winning so much in their favour that it was almost mathematically impossible to win. But when someone did figure out a way to beat them, they usually not only won, they won big.

No surprise then that Nickolas and Techno, now miraculously recovered from their bout of tiredness, had dropped in to try their luck[51].

"And the winner is — electronic drum roll — Number 888," the casino dealer announced. At this, Techno and Nickolas shrieked with joy and gave each other another high-five. "You bloody beauty! How many credits have we won now?" Techno cried, jumping up and down, much to the annoyance of the other gambling patrons.

---

[50] Like the game called 'Power Ironing' where you have limited time to iron two hundred shirts, or you get branded — on your backside no less — by the very same device.

[51] And by luck, I mean Techno's lightning-fast reflexes and ability to count e-cards by the million.

"Enough to keep us in cocktails for quite some time Tech." Nickolas grinned as another pile of winning chips came there way.

"Gentleman," the floor manager interrupted. "Congratulations on your ridiculous run of good luck." This was said in the sort of tone you would use if your best friend had won the Intergalactic Lottery jackpot but still insisted you pay back those few credits you borrowed off them some time ago.

"Thanks, mate," Techno replied, as he slipped his hand into the floor manager's back pocket and continued the run of 'ridiculous good luck.'

"We are pleased to offer you a complimentary night-cycle's stay in one of our deluxe penthouse suites for you to relax and unwind," — *while we study the camera recordings to see how you screwed us.* "We look forward to taking excellent care of you," — *right up to the point we have local law enforcement arrest you.*

"Lead the way, kind sir," Nickolas said. "I think we both deserve a nice massage after a hard cycle or so making a small fortune. This will give you a chance to empty your pockets too, Tech," he said, slapping him on the back, and inadvertently dislodging a bunch of chips Techno had liberated from other patron's pockets up and down the casino pit.

The floor manager shook his head and said, "Riff raff … I wish you *could* beat them."

***

Meanwhile, Xymod, Nerada, and Jonathan slowly navigated their way across the busy city. The city was made up of a giant jungle of gambling pits and over-engineered hotels. It had achieved the precise lack of class and taste the designers were aspiring to. Every nationality of Qurkition was represented, and many from other galaxies. Xymod, led the way, and apparently didn't need directions. This was strange, as he claimed he hadn't set foot on this planet for some time.

"It's ruddy ironic," Jonathan commented as they walked, "that most planets will go to war with each other at a moment's notice, over as little as an unpaid docking fine. However, bring everyone together with the chance of winning a quick credit, in any one of these jolly gambling establishments, and it's the most peaceful planet in the system."

"Greed is what greed does, brother," Nerada replied looking rather pleased with herself.

"Oh, indeed," Jonathan said, with a slight grin on his face.

They continued to walk through the maze of buildings which, occasionally, were broken up by an expensively priced mobile cocktail bar or a big neon sign pointing towards the next casino.

After a few more moments, Xymod stopped and looked around.

"Hello, brother," a voice behind Jonathan and Nerada said.

"Hello, Xyrapt," Xymod said, reaching forward, a warm smile on his face. This greeting was a weird gesture neither Jonathan nor Nerada had seen before.

The brothers turned towards Nerada and Jonathan. "Your friends?" Xyrapt asked.

"Yes. May I introduce Nerada and Jonathan Milarum.

"Glad to make your acquaintances," said Xyrapt, who could pass as the spitting image of Xymod in every way except for his over-the-top, blue-themed attire and bright blue hair.

Xyrapt looked upon Nerada. "Welcome to you especially, my young lady." He bent and kissed her on the hand.

"Why thank you," Nerada replied, a slight blush crept to her face.

"Come, my friends. Let's retire from the heat and take refreshment," Xyrapt said, as he led them down an alley. It opened into a huge courtyard, attached to the biggest house Nerada and Jonathan had ever seen. After they had been seated in one of the courtyard's many gazebos, and appropriate refreshments had been served, they were able to take in the magnificent view of the back garden.

"So, brother, what brings you to my humble abode?" Xyrapt asked.

"This." Xymod took the Amulet from his pocket. He wasn't in the mood for any more small talk.

Xyrapt froze. His demeanour transformed into something more serious. He gestured to Xymod to take a stroll with him around the grounds. When next they exchanged words, it was in a strange language even Jonathan and Nerada's SUTS[52] could not make heads or tails of. After listening to the two brothers locked in deep discussion for a while, which was heated at times, Nerada leaned over to Jonathan. "Maybe my SUTS needs updating, can you understand a word of this?"

"Unfortunately, not old girl. It sounds remarkably like an old language though. Extremely old."

"How do you know?"

"Without wanting to confuse you too much with linguistic mumbo jumbo, it's because it is being spoken by those two old codgers over there," Jonathan pointed in the general direction of

---

[52] The Subrium Universal Translator Strain (SUTS) is a virus baked into every sentient species DNA in the universe. Certainly not an exact or even safe science, it does, though, allow most beings to communicate with almost all other beings MOST of the time. None more so than Apop Spop of Pertion 89, who spent so much time updating his SUTS via the SUTS comms channel that he barely ever had time to leave his house to test the upgrades. Thankfully, he did put his fully updated SUTS to use that sun-cycle when an armed robber broke into his house, put a ConVoser to his head, and pointed to Apop's wall safe.

Xymod and his brother.

"Thanks for your expert explanation," Nerada remarked blandly. The brothers continued to converse for some time, until Xymod bid farewell to Xyrapt with a warm hug. He returned to his companions and they started walking back in the general direction of their ship.

"So, does your brother have the Shard, old bean?"

"No. However, he did tell me where it is. It is currently being accommodated by the Gas Giants."

"Will he assist in its retrieval?"

"No, although he will not stop us either. He supports our quest. Xyrapt senses the danger of the Zarnegy. However, it's the Shard itself that will decide if it wants to leave the planet. Not him."

"Not wanting to state the obvious then," Nerada said, "but what happens if the Shard isn't in the mood for a trip to wherever the hell we are headed? What then?"

"We will cross that meedy[53] if we come to it," muttered Xymod, now deep in thought.

Xymod, Jonathan, and Nerada returned smartly to the to find, (surprise, surprise) no sign of the boys. M011y, now hooked up into the planet's central network, was scanning all system traffic for any sign of them.

"I ruddy knew it," Jonathan said, shaking his head. "Let's jolly well hope it's not too expensive to spring them from the cell they're both probably dwelling in by now."

"If that's a cell, remind me to get locked up in one of them on my next vacation," Nerada said, as M011y displayed the boys on her primary screen. It showed a live feed of Nickolas and

---

[53] Similar to a bridge but has a toll tax so high that no one ever crosses it, in fear of becoming instantly insolvent.

Techno enjoying a rub down while sipping cocktails in what looked like one of the casino's penthouse suites.

"Grrr," Jonathan growled as he picked up his communicator and made his way back off the ship.

"Note to oneself. Next time, roll with those two," Nerada murmured to herself as she and Xymod followed him.

9. Timmy

"YOU KNOW MY RULE ABOUT HAVING FULLY ARMED DOMESTIC COMPANIONS IN THE HOUSE, DON'T YOU?"

The *Aletheia* was making good time as it sped Thomas and Eloise visHamogus to Aertion 82 for an impromptu meeting with Thomas's old school friend, Felicity Milarum. Too good a time, Thomas thought, as he wasn't having much luck convincing his sister that his plan to wangle information out of Felicity was watertight.

"I am simply not going to do it, brother," Eloise shouted, around the same time a flying bottle nearly hit him square in the face. Luckily for Thomas, he'd had plenty of practice dodging flying objects from Eloise over the cycles and evaded it easily.

"I mean, you and Daddy blackmail me into coming on this pointless little venture, on your grotty little ship, to visit some Milarum horror on some crummy little planet. As if this isn't bad enough, you want me to pretend to be that sad git Jonathan Milarum's 'concerned' girlfriend?"

"Not entirely, Eloise." He now braced for the worst. "You aren't exactly his 'concerned' girlfriend. The long and short of it is … you're the mother of his child."

"What! You're a Bertion 12 Getta[54] short of a rotten picnic if you think Felicity Milarum will fall for that!"

"Why not? Didn't you once go on a date with him?"

"Yes, about an eon ago, and I loathed every moment of it. Especially at the end of the night-cycle when the posh git had the

---

[54] A giant sandwich, and I mean huge.

audacity to try to hold my hand."

"The nerve," Thomas replied, looking amused.

"Anyway, Doctor Brainbox, aren't you missing a key ingredient to your two-bit plan, for example, an actual kid?"

"No, not at all." Thomas reached inside his jacket and pulled out a tiny device. "May I present to you … your son." He pressed a button and a small child appeared in front of Eloise, causing her to jump back in surprise.

Thomas laughed. "His name is Timmy, and he loves his mummy greatly."

"You have got to be joking."

"He's the newest form of hologram technology made by our boffins on Certion 18. Totally programmable and life-like. I mixed yours and Milarum's DNA, which one of our spy-bugs collected, to make the little charger look even more legit."

"Mummy! Mummy!" Timmy cried. He sprang forward and hugged Eloise's leg. "How I love you so!"

"You owe me, brother. You owe me, big time!" Eloise spat, as she tried to get her holographic son off her leg.

To Thomas's relief the conversation was interrupted by his ship's main computer, Sama1tha.

"Well th1s grotty little 5hip is now approach1ng that crummy l1ttle p1anet. Thought u 5hould know," she said, with more than a little hint of sarcasm.

"Great. Thanks Sam," Thomas said, making his way from his sister's quarters and back towards his own. "Please request landing permission. Please also request an audience with Felicity Milarum, as a matter of urgency."

A few moments later, Sama1tha replied with, "Permiss1on granted to land in docking bay 4, and the 'horror' has agre3d 2 meet u 5hortly."

"Roger that." Now all he needed was to figure out what to wear.

Shortly after landing, the visHamogus siblings were escorted to Felicity's office by Fredrick and Matilda.

Little Timmy tried to pick up and cuddle poor Fredrick the entire journey. "Mummy! Mummy! Can I keep him?" Timmy shouted, as he made another unsuccessful grab for Fredrick.

"No Timmy," Eloise said. "You know my rule about having fully armed domestic companions in the house, don't you?"

They found Felicity sitting in her favourite chair, intently studying something on one of her console screens.

After being shown to their seats, Fredrick left the room, much to the disappointment of Timmy. Matilda took up position behind the visHamogus siblings on one of the many surrounding couches and scrutinised them closely.

"Greetings, ex-school colleagues. To what do I owe the pleasure? Oh, and you brought a delightful little child too. How positively divine of you," Felicity said in a satirical tone[55].

"It's delightful to see you too, dearest Felly," — an old school nickname for Felicity that she positively despised, and Eloise knew it — Eloise said between clinched teeth.

"So," Thomas interrupted, as he saw Eloise was quickly losing her cool, "It's a delicate situation, unfortunately. We were hoping we could locate your brother, Jonathan."

"Oh, and why would that be?" Felicity replied, becoming more suspicious by the moment.

---

[55] Although highly intelligent and strikingly attractive in figure, Felicity had never found any real use for relationships or children of her own. Other than her work, she didn't live for much else. This positively suited her, as having screaming kids and/or partners spilling something or other on the rare material that no doubt graced her latest XYZ luxury possession wasn't what she would consider 'a swimmingly good time.'

"The core of the matter is that young Timmy here is more than the beloved child of my sister. He is also the child of your brother … Yes, Felicity," he said, leaning back in his chair, at the same time slipping a small device out of his pocket and dropping it down the back of his seat, "Timmy here is your nephew. Congratulations."

Timmy sprung into life and started shouting, "Aunty Felly! Aunty Felly!"

At this news, even Felicity was taken aback for a split flash. But she regained her composure and sat staring at Timmy.

"Yes, we have had the appropriate tests done, and it's confirmed," Thomas continued. "He even has the Milarum nose, as you can see. So, it is only fair that we inform your brother immediately, so he can make arrangements."

"Okay, Thomas," Felicity said, now fully recovering her poise. "You can shut up and let your sister talk. So why now?" Felicity asked Eloise. "Why after all this time?"

"Because, my dear Felly, I think it only fair for the young boy to know the truth and to have a chance to get to know his real father. It's also tough being a single, working mother in this cycle's cruel galaxy."

"Single, working mother? You haven't worked a cycle in your entire life, Eloise visHamogus. And I don't buy your story for even half a moment. It's obvious you two are up to something."

"Oh, that is a little harsh, Felicity," Thomas said. He reached across and stopped his sister from pulling out her ConVoser-1. "We did come here in good faith, and for old time's sake. I mean, even our parents worked closely together for all those cycles."

"Indeed. Until your father backstabbed my father[56] and took full ownership of the company our mothers started together."

"Business is business, Felicity. Who truly knows the real doings of mice and mechanoids," Thomas replied.

"Okay, Thomas Michael visHamogus, enough of your pointless gobbledygook …" Felicity was eager to wrap things up and go back to her other, more urgent, business.

"Fair enough, and as you said, 'for old times' sake'. The next time I see Jonathan, I will let him know and request that he reaches out to you."

"So, you don't know where he is?" Thomas enquired.

"No, I'm afraid not. I haven't seen him for a lunar-cycle. Last I heard he was doing his utmost to destroy as much public property as possible, while making IAFE pick up the bill. Now, you must excuse me," Felicity said bluntly, as she turned her attention back to her console. "I have plenty to be getting on with."

"Fair enough, Felicity," Thomas said. The three of them made their way to the door. "Thanks for your time. It was great to see you again. We should catch up again one sun-cycle and talk about old times."

"Yes. Sure. Why not?" she said with a genuine hint of sincerity.

"Oh, and Thomas?"

"Yes?"

---

[56] The Milarum and visHamogus families where once quite close, brought together by the friendship and business concerns of Oliver and Franklin's wives — Josephine Milarum and Omelia visHamogus. Oliver and Franklin, on the other hand, didn't see eye to eye on much at all. So, when Omelia, Franklin's wife and mother to Thomas and Eloise, passed away from a rare illness, followed soon after by the mysterious disappearance of Josephine Milarum, Franklin affected a hostile takeover of the business and turned the once not-for-profit rare animal protection charity into an all-for-profit ConVoser small arms manufactory.

"I think you've forgotten something."

"Oh, whatever do you mean?" he retorted, looking as innocent as a visHamogus could[57].

"This," she said, throwing him the device he'd tried to plant in the chair. Matilda had spotted it, dug it out, and handed it to Felicity.

"Oh, thanks," he said. "I'm always losing that."

"Yes, I bet you are," Felicity said, smiling tightly.

"Matilda," Felicity said as soon as the visHamogus siblings had left. "Please locate my brothers and patch me through to them immediately. I get the distinct feeling that we aren't the only ones looking for the Octarm Amulet and Shards."

"Yeah, I think u are right there dude," Matilda said, as she hurried off to communications.

***

The visHamogus siblings, now back on their ship, took off immediately. As soon as they were in orbit, they contacted their father.

"She's up to something all right," Eloise said.

"Oh, I don't doubt that for a flash, although that is of no concern now. I have received information as to her brother's whereabouts and will be sending some business associates to take care of the situation," Franklin replied.

"And who might these associates be?" Thomas asked. He was all too aware of his father's reputation when it came to resolving situations.

"The Pretubo sisters"

"You tell those crazy nut jobs to stay put until I get back," Thomas said. "I plan on tagging along."

---

[57] About a 3 out of 10, at best.

Thomas terminated the communication with his father, then glanced at his sister.

"Oh no brother. You can count me out. And anyway I am a single mother and as such have some serious drinking to catchup up on," Eloise knew that glance and wanted no part of it.

"Fair enough. Sama1tha. Get us back home. Sharpish."

10. The Emergency Intergalactic Transport Device

"IT WILL BE A CASE OF SHOOT FIRST, THINK LATER ... MUCH LATER."

The penthouse suite that Nickolas and the prince were offered for relaxing in was in keeping with the rest of the Grand Cutthroat Corsair Casino — preposterously large and decorated with the same space-pirate theme as the main casino floor. As if that wasn't bad enough, the interior designers and decorators obviously had some sickening fascination with the most famous space-pirate of them all — Big Long Bong Buck[58]. The suite had around one thousand e-photos of him plastered all over the walls.

Not even noticing the decorations, Prince Techno and Nickolas wasted no time in putting on the complementary pirate-themed eye patch, which was VR enabled and allowed them to order room service without lifting a finger. The pair, not

---

[58] Big Long Bong Buck was famous in the Lertion System for his meticulously planned space-pirate attacks on space freighters. It was almost seen as a spot of fun when he boarded your ship and demanded to see the cargo hold. This was mainly because Big Long Bong Buck was only ever after rum, which was by far the least popular form of liquor in the system. Hence in the four solar cycles he operated, Big Long Bong Buck illegally boarded several ships, but he only ever found a cargo hold full of rum once, and that freighter was lost. Unfortunately, so excited was he by this discovery that he ended up drinking himself to death.

knowing what they fancied, simply ordered one of everything on the menu and then started emptying out the contents of their pockets onto one of the huge tables, which was fittingly shaped in the form of a treasure chest.

"Mate, what does this do again?" Techno asked, picking up a small, square shaped device with a big, red button on it.

"Hold it, Tech! I strongly advise you to NOT press that button. Not unless you want to find yourself randomly transported to some far-flung place." Nickolas was used to the prince pretty much helping himself to anything he wanted, whenever it suited him. It was his culture, after all.

"So, what does it do again, mate?" Techno repeated, fighting with every fibre of his being to NOT press the button, while not listening to a word Nickolas was saying.

"That, my little green companion, is my Emergency Intergalactic Transport Device or EITD for short. This little gadget has liberated me from plenty a pickle over the cycles. Especially over disagreements with bartenders and restaurant owners about economic remuneration for rudimentary goods and services."

"Yes, they do get bloody touchy about that sort of nonsense, don't they?" Techno had made a career out of paying for bugger all.

"Only problem is it can only transport up to two people at a time, so not much help when you're out with a bunch of friends at some dodgy establishment and require a hasty exit. Luckily, I don't have any friends," Nickolas said, in a surprisingly proud tone.

"Oh, yeah. I remember now. You used it once on that mongrel trade merchant." Techno casually handed the device back to Nickolas and continued to count the credits they had acquired both legally, but mostly illegally, on the casino floor. "Who did you bloody liberate it from again?"

"I didn't. It was a gift from my father. He gave my brother the *Beletheia* and he gave me this little gizmo. I'm not bitter about it," he said, in a bitter tone. "At least he remembered our birth-cycles that time. However, more importantly than all that, Tech, what type of back rub should I get next? Deep tissue or trigger point?"

"How about the golly gosh 'get off my flipping backside and help figure out a plan to obtain the first Shard?' massage," Jonathan said in an annoyed tone, as he, Nerada, and Xymod entered the hotel suite. A suite now littered with numerous empty bubbly wine bottles, half-eaten boxes of the extremely expensive 'eat-yourself-to-a-thinner-you' luxury chocolates, and huge piles of casino currency.

"This is an absolute disgrace," Nerada said, with more than a little bit of jealousy in her voice. She poured herself a glass of bubbly.

"Yes, yes. All in good time. I mean, these guys aren't cheap, and we did pay for the entire cycle you know," Nickolas said, motioning to the four masseuses currently working on him to step it up a bit. "And another thing—"

Before Nickolas could fully launch into his latest conspiracy theory about the massage industry, and how they massage stress-knots into your lower back purely to secure repeat business — present company excluded of course — he was interrupted by Commy, who informed them of an urgent incoming communication.

"It's not my bookie, is it?" Nickolas asked. "If it is, please inform him we are currently unavailable due to the following reasons:

Reason 1 — that last 'sure thing' tip he gave me on some slug race on Certion 6, pretty much put me in so much debt that my great-grandchildren will still be making the interest payments.

Reason 2 — As such, if I ever lay eyes on his ugly mug again, it will be a case of shoot first, think later ... much later.

Reason 3 — Please refer to reason two."

A massive holographic figure lit up in the middle of the room, engulfing it completely.

"No, you poor excuse for a salad-dodging oxygen thief. It's little, ole Felly, your long-suffering older sister," Felicity said.

"Oh, stuffing, blasted buggery, with knobs on," Nickolas moaned. "I almost wished it was my bookie now."

"Glad to see you sacrificing yourself for the cause, Nickolas." She looked scornfully down at him, lying flat on his stomach, while sipping on his 14th Aertion12OnTheRocks[59] cocktail.

"Absolutely. The stress of being the people's poet does tax one."

"Well, I hate to rain on your parade, however, I've just transferred to M011y all the information we found on the CRAP database concerning the Black Mist, the Zarnegy, and the last known whereabouts of our father. It's a little thin, although I will continue studying it to see if any of the information is useful. Xymod, could you please have a look at the data?"

"My pleasure," Xymod replied. He was still a little more thoughtful than usual after visiting his brother. "Your father sent the package from a planet which is not known to me. Hence, I'm guessing he didn't find the Amulet on it. It's extremely

---

[59] The Aertion12OnTheRocks cocktail was made famous as the recipe included an actual small rock from the planet's surface. So popular in fact, they had to start importing small rocks from the neighbouring planets just to keep up with demand.

interesting."

"Is there anything to report at your end, other than the lack of contents in the mini-bar?"

"My brother has told me his Shard is currently accommodated by the Gas Giants and has been residing with them for generations. I doubt they'll give it up lightly. *But every path has its puddles.*"

"Oh," Felicity said, "a tricky bunch of characters from what I've heard. Not the most welcoming of sorts. Keep me informed of your progress. I'll have Matilda send you over any intelligence we have on them. Again, I doubt it will help much."

"Jolly good," Jonathan said. "I have a feeling we'll need all the assistance we can get with these Gas Giant folk."

"On other matters," Felicity continued, "I've had a random visit from our old school chums Thomas visHamogus and his sister, Eloise. Let's assume they're tangled up in this somehow, along with that insane father of theirs. Be careful of anything to do with the visHamogus family, starting with that casino, you morons. They own it, hence it won't take them long to find you."

"Why?" Jonathan said. "It's not as though they can ruddy arrest us."

"You're right there," Felicity said. "However, that appears to be the least of your issues, Jonathan Oliver Milarum."

"Issues? What do you mean 'issues', old girl?"

"Dear brother, it appears Eloise wants a friendly chat with you sometime."

"Eloise visHamogus? I haven't seen her in ages … what would she golly gosh want to talk to me about?"

"Let's say you two have a little package of joy to discuss. Apparently, you're a father, and that professional drunk, Eloise visHamogus, is the mother."

"I'm a ruddy what!" Jonathan cried out, with a mixture of both surprise and panic.

"He's a what?" the rest of the group said, with expressions ranging from bemusement to downright amusement.

Jonathan was already heading for the door. "Righty-oh then ladies and gents, you heard Felicity. Show time is over. Let's get bloody well moving, shall we?"

"Yes, indeed. Spiffing and toodle-pip, brother," Nickolas said, in his poshest accent. "Time is credits on this deal, and this man now has a family to feed."

"Oh, and Nerada," Felicity said. "I'm not sure how you ended up there, and which part of 'monitor your brothers' you didn't get. Next time I see you, dear little sister, we'll have a nice long chat."

"Don't worry, Nerada," Nickolas butted in. "You may be about to get fired, but given you're probably going to be target practice for some Gas Giant shortly." He winked at Techno. "By my calculations, you will most probably be dead by brunch anyway."

"Bonza, mate!" Techno cried, as he gave Nickolas another of those annoying high fives. "You're on fire this cycle, cobber."

"No ... not yet he isn't. Although that can certainly be arranged," Felicity concluded before terminating the communication.

11. Harold 'The Beast' Booting

"IT'S OKAY, THE MORE I EAT, THE FATTER I GET."

Gwendolyn and Romeo's ship landed on Aertion 12 around late-sun-cycle local time. The QLEB officers wasted no time going about their business in trying to track down the Milarum party. Their first stop was the local law enforcement outpost, which was under the command of Captain Harold 'The Beast' Booting.

"My esteemed colleagues, what brings the QLEB fishing in my pool this cycle?" The Beast said. He looked at Gwendolyn and Romeo, who were now sitting in his unkempt office, thinking it would be a cold cycle in hell before they put The Beast's massive luncheon — which he had now started — of deep-fried chocolate Fubu[60], raw pear, and red pumpkin on the menu of their own restaurants.

"Ourrr mission is a simple locate and abstrrract, Captain. Herrre arrre ourrr orrrderrrs," Gwendolyn said as she opened her carry bag and pulled out a long, flat e-tablet. She verified herself via DNA recognition and placed it on The Beast's desk so he could corroborate their orders.

"Who are you after?" He asked as he took another bite of his Fubu, without even glancing at the device.

"A few layabouts. Layabouts vho arrre in desperrrate need of some rrreflection time in one of ourrr maximum securrrity

---

[60] Imagine a doughnut with no hole in the middle, filled with mustard that smells like a raw pork chop.

cells," Gwendolyn replied.

"You have certainly come to the right place then. Most of this planet's population could do with a little reflection time in one of our prison cells. Who are the lucky souls soon to be on holicycle? I might be able to assist you in locating them."

"A-Jonathan-and-Nickolas-Milarum-plus-party-BEEP-BEEP," Romeo said.

"Oh, those two. Easy. One of them was being monitored in one of the casino's hotels. Apparently, he and his little green chum have been fleecing the gambling establishment, via non-ethical methods. Obviously, they're going to be either arrested or, in most cases, offered a job."

"Tat vould be Nickolas, no doubt, and I have a fairrr idea vho his little grrreen frrriend is too."

"We were about to drag them in for questioning. However, they left the hotel earlier without a trace."

"Do-you-know-where-they-might-be-heading-BEEP-BEEP?"

"Not sure. Although you're welcome to review the hotel recordings of the room. It might turn something up." The Beast prepared to start eating a dessert so big it could moonlight as a small planet.

Gwendolyn and Romeo stood. "Yes. Ve vill starrrt terrre, thank you."

"I'll have one of my people show you to our central casino security recording department."

"Thankyou-Captain-and-you-have-yourself-an-above-average-sun-cycle-Oh-and-between-you-and-I-you-should-attempt-to-cut-back-on-your-calorie-intake-I-have-calculated-your-dessert-it's-around-the-same-recommended-daily-allowance-of-an-entire-village-BEEP-BEEP."

"It's okay, the more I eat, the fatter I get," The Beast retorted, as if this were the breakthrough that had been perplexing nutritionists for eons[61].

"Oh, and one last thing valued colleagues. Purely because I am allowing you to fish in my pool doesn't mean you can piss in it. So try not to break too much while you're snooping around. And let me know when you've located them. Your reputation does precede you."

"Juniorrr Qurrrkition Space Cadet prrromise," Gwendolyn said, as she gave him the now infamous Jr. Qurkition Space Cadet salute.

He nodded. "Cute."

As the two QLEB officers left his office, he considered how most of the organised crime and mayhem conducted throughout the galaxy was usually orchestrated by former Jr. Qurkition Space Cadets. Hence, he didn't hold out much hope that this was going to end well — for anyone.

Gwendolyn and Romeo were led directly to one of the viewing rooms, and commenced reviewing Nickolas and Techno's hotel room security footage.

Initially all they were subjected to was a bunch of idle chit-chat where Nickolas was trying to explain, in detail, the finer art of a backwards defensive batting stroke. This was while they were both getting rubdowns, while watching the 87th cycle of a local Cimmick[62] match through their VR eye-patches. Romeo

---

[61] Then again, perplexing Qurkition nutritionists wasn't all that hard. Half of their profession was recently wiped out at their annual galactic conference after trying a suggestion left on one of their feedback surveys, which claimed a strict diet of one teaspoon of capsicum mixed with one litre of Nxxcop — think arsenic, only worse ... much worse — every cycle for a solar-cycle would immediately solve galactic obesity rates in adults. This event confirmed the galactic-wide assumption that if you say the word 'gullible' slowly enough it sounds like 'nutritionist.'

[62] Like cricket, but played in slow motion, and with two hundred players each side.

commented to Gwendolyn that if he had to sit through any more of this gibberish, he would be tempted to hit his own self-destruct button.

"Arrre you surrre ve have ze rrright rrroom?" Gwendolyn said, somewhat bemused. "Because if tese simpletons arrre ze folks after ze Amulet of Octarrrm, I tink ve can pack up nov and go home. Perrrfectly safe in ze knovledge tat, even if ze legend existed, tese idiots vould have about as much chance of finding it, as Rrreeto Kveento[63]."

In response, Romeo told the pesky hotel security computer to find something useful in the Nickolas and Techno room recordings, or it was going to have more to worry about than constantly warning them about 'protecting the privacy of our patrons,' like being e-arrested and dismantled for wasting QLEB officers' time.

Unsurprisingly, moments later, the security computer found the information they were interested in, and the QLEB officers listened intently to Felicity's message, and Xymod's findings, which outlined the Milarum's next move.

"Afterrr all tat banging on, tey arrre heading to ze Rrrealm of ze Gas Giants?"

"Appears-that-way-let's-also-pay-them-a-visit-shall-we-

---

[63] Reeto Kweento was the most famous treasure hunter in Qurkition. He had it all: six large continent estates, twelve supercharged Ferriopolia hyper-craft, and as much banana cake as his chubby little cheeks could eat. The only slight issue for Reeto was that although he was blessed with the best Marketing and PR department in the known galaxy, he wasn't, in the strictest sense, a treasure hunter at all. So once the news broke that Reeto had outsourced his entire treasure hunting operation to a small contractor on Omertion 17 — they also did dry cleaning and shoe repair — his PR department, as you can imagine, had to kick into major damage control. You'll be glad to know that Reeto recovered from this little setback and ended up starting his own consulting and training business, assisting Gertion 1 with important government business. As he used to say, "If you're not part of the solution, there is good money to be made prolonging the problem." All strictly off the record, of course. The exciting news is he didn't have to sell even one of his Ferriopolias in the end. I don't know about you, but this makes my heart sing.

BEEP-BEEP."

"Does yourrr data-storrre have any inforrrmation on tese Gas Giants?" Gwendolyn asked, as they briskly headed back to their craft.

"Afraid-not-partner-but-I-would-assume-they-are-giants-and-they-have-something-going-on-with-gas-BEEP-BEEP."

"And you deducted tat all by yourrrself? Astonishing vorrrk detective!"

"Shall-we-inform-Captain-Booting-where-we-are-going?-BEEP-BEEP."

They boarded their ship and fired up the engines.

"No need to boter captain monsterrr munch yet. I tink he vill have enough on his plate trrrying to digest tat banquet he gorrrged himself on forrr supper. Nov, let's get moving."

12. The Cosmic Realm of the Gas Giants

"TAKING NO CHANCES IN THE, 'OH DEAR, I DIDN'T BRING ENOUGH IN THE FIREPOWER' DEPARTMENT'."

It was early in the sun-cycle when the *Beletheia* landed a safe distance away from the Gas Giants capital city, Gasstro. They chose a secluded location, near the edge of a huge forest. Jonathan suggested it would be the height of bad manners to simply barge in before the suns were even up, so the companions waited for the first signs of light. This suited Nickolas and Techno as they had plenty of time to fit in a few more CosmicCourage! cocktails[64].

"M011y, old girl, you might want to cloak yourself once we head off, as we might be some time. I'd also say we will more than likely have some unfriendly company in tow when, or for that matter if, we make it back."

His tone sounded a bit too dramatic for Mo11y's liking.

"What? R you planning on perform1ng your 'act' while u r there, r u?" M011y rebutted rudely.

They spent the next few moments gearing up, with Techno, Nickolas, and Nerada taking no chances in the 'Oh dear, I didn't bring enough in the firepower' department. After finally being

---

[64] Packed with enough hard liquor to make even the timidest of beings "cosmically" brave. It was the "*FTW!*" element (usually a 200% pure hot air self-motivational chemically induced ramble) that helped convince yourself you were going to make it when you most clearly were not.

hurried up by Jonathan, the now over-armed companions left the *Beletheia*. They started walking down what vaguely resembled a dirt path, which led in the general direction of the city.

"D0n't forget where Ur're parked, folks, as I w1ll n0t be able 2 communicate wh1le 1 am cloaked," M011y reminded them.

"Jolly good," Jonathan replied. "Our communicators will guide us back."

"Oh, and don't do anyth1ng 1 wouldn't d0," M011y said, as she cloaked the *Beletheia*.

"Don't worry, M011y, I intend on doing as little as possible," Nickolas said.

"Situation normal then?" Nerada said smugly, as she walked past him.

"This is a classic smash and grab job, cobbers," Techno stated. "If we hit them dead on, guns blazing, we'll certainly bloody surprise them, and while they are off-guard, Nerada and Nickolas here will give the king both barrels, while I grab the bloody Shard and sod off. Job well and bloody done."

"Oh, what a spiffingly excellent plan," Jonathan said, shaking his head. "Rest assured, my little friend, we will be right behind you the entire way. Around twenty miles behind you to be exact. Now, let's jolly well get real and figure out a real strategy. Anyone else want to take a shot?"

"Considering we have Xymod, I thought it would be obvious. We march in there, ask for the Shard, and when they refuse, let Xymod give them a new definition of the word bloodbath," Nickolas said.

Jonathan awarded him with an above average eyeroll.

"While I appreciate your sound theory," Xymod said, "and *sometimes a spark can create a great fire*. Unfortunately, I have little 'bloodbath' power away from my home planet. I will be able to give us only limited protection, but not much else. My brother, on the other hand—"

"I guess we'll have to rely on a strategy that doesn't involve going in all ConVoser's blazing, and use our experience, intellect, and creativity instead," Nerada said.

"Great, and here's me thinking things couldn't get any worse," Nickolas replied.

The companions continued to walk towards the city, discussing their strategy for obtaining the Shard as they went. The information that Matilda sent through on the Gas Giants was thin. But it did confirm the race was about as inhospitable as the famous Shhipy family of Dertion 5[65].

This situation wasn't made any better for them when, in between a lot more walking, a spot more arguing, and a bunch of threats of what would befall Techno if he volunteered even one more master plan, the Milarum party suddenly stumbled out of the woods and found themselves smack bang in front of Gasstro's massive city gates. These gates looked both extremely uninviting and firmly shut. The surrounding stone walls, which encircled and protected the entire Gas Giant city, weren't shouting 'welcome weary traveller,' either.

The group, all feeling a little bit exposed, and still minus a plan that didn't involve a bunch of wild ConVoser fire and even wilder assumptions, slowly started to back away from the gates.

Everyone, but Xymod mind you, who, before anyone could

---

[65] The Shhipy family owned and operated a hotel on Dertion 5. Not a small hotel, mind you, but a massive complex which included 56,000 rooms, four hundred swimming pools, eight hundred and ninety restaurants and so many shops, there was even one which specialised entirely in rubber bands. It's surprising then, that in the three solar-cycles the Shhipy family owned the establishment, they failed to ever take one booking. The hotel, it's said, ran so efficiently that Mrs Shhipy was not going to have the inconvenience of an actual guest mess with the calm equilibrium of the place.

do anything to stop him, stepped forward and introduced himself to the two Gas Giants guarding the gates and kindly requested a meeting with their king.

"It's simple. I will explain the situation. And if the king has an ounce of common sense, he'll hand over the Shard and we will be on our way. *Where there's a will there's a way*," Xymod concluded, as the front gates opened, and more than a few Gas Giant guards poured out from Gasstro and surrounded them. "Honesty, after all, is the best policy." For Xymod, this was a way of life, and the logical path to take. To the rest of the galaxy though, this path was a bunch of cobblers.

Geffkl Deennu was a proud Giant. He was 12-foot-tall, which was tall, even for a Gas Giant. The King of the Gas Giants prided himself on being a fair and ethical ruler, with a pinch of good, old-fashioned kindness thrown in for good measure. He loved his people, and they loved him back. Why wouldn't they? His family had ruled throughout the centuries with such fairness that he was most probably the fairest and most selfless leader since King Olap Nvvn of Etertion 9[66].

Unfortunately for his subjects, and everyone else he ever had dealings with, the dream he was having — or nightmare in Geffkl's case — ended when a knock on his chamber door jarred him awake.

"Fair and ethical?" he said to himself, as he climbed out of bed, grabbed his royal crested robe from his wardrobe, and made his way to the door. "Not on my watch."

---

[66] King Nvvn was a king who took it so personally that some of his subjects lived in poverty and squalor while he lived in luxury, that he abdicated his throne and gave all his personal fortune to the realm's sick and needy. It's a crying shame really that his son and sole heir didn't feel the same way on this subject. This was confirmed by his first order of business as king, which was a royal command to round up all the realm's beggars, homeless and poor — which included his father at this point — and sent them on a one-way fact-finding mission into the nearest sun.

"So'ry to distu'wbyah, oh holy one. Howevah, we have some outsidah's who have requested an audience," came the words of Auffi, his closest advisor and sycophant.

"Outsidah's, huh? We don't often get them. I wondah what they want?"

"They didn't say. Shall we g'want them an audience?"

"Fine, why not? I could do with a laugh, right up to the point I th'wow them into the dungeons," Geffkl said with a hint of satisfaction in his voice.

The companions, now having access to the city, were escorted to the royal palace by the king's personal guard. Gasstro palace was impressive in size and stature. The royal palace, easily the biggest building in the city, was located in the middle of the capital, right on the top of a hill. This large, gold-coloured, hand-crafted, stone fortress shone brightly in the early-sun-cycle suns.

The palace overlooked Gasstro city, which was made up of thousands of large, red-stoned buildings of all shapes and sizes. It had wide, brown-stoned cobbled streets, and numerous well-appointed public squares filled with markets, all teeming with Gas Giants going about their business — or whatever it was they did. The city was beautiful except for its odour. Spread throughout the city were many holes in the ground that spewed out gas of such a foul stench it made the entire city smell worse than the biggest dumping ground of the galaxy, the planet Kertion 4[67]. This was unfortunate for Nerada, who had an extremely keen sense of smell — and for anyone else with an even a partially working nose, and to make matter worse for

---

[67] The same Kertion 4 that now regretted using the phrase 'your trash is our treasure' as their planet's motto, because trash— in every sense of the word, and in reality — was trash, and treasure couldn't possibly smell as repugnant as the last dumping runs made by the giant, mega-trash transport crafts from Gertion 45.

Nickolas, the smell seemed to sober him up.

The companions were escorted into the huge royal palace court. With ridiculously large, stone carvings of fierce looking Gas Giants lining the walls, and a ceiling made entirely of glass, the massive room could easily have passed as a modern night-cycle rave club, especially given the amount of gas being released from random holes in the floor coupled with the booming electronic dance music reverberating from every angle.

"This joint reminds me of my local discotheque back home," Nickolas commented.

They were led further into the vast room, until they came upon a figure sitting on a stone carved throne. The throne was huge, with intricate carvings encrusted with multiple jewels. One jewel fashioned into the throne was of specific interest to Xymod. To the seated Giant's left stood another Giant, who was obviously some sort of advisor.

"Greetings Collector," a voice from within Xymod's head said as he looked at the deep, red Shard. It was so magnificent, beautiful in colour, cut, and shape, it almost brought him to tears of both admiration and relief.

"Greetings, Vigor, beloved Shard of Octarm. I come with grave news of impending danger," Xymod said telepathically.

"Yes, I sense the peril. It is time."

"My friends," Xymod whispered to the companions, as he pointed to the Shard on the king's throne. "Behold Vigor, Octarm's primordial Shard of Energy."

The companions couldn't hide the fact that they were all a little excited.

"But the jewel is huge," Nickolas said. "There's no way it will fit into that Amulet of yours."

"Have faith, Nickolas. It will when the time is right," Xymod replied in a self-assured manner.

"Outsidah's," barked King Geffkl's advisor, Auffi. "Why do you bothah his holyniss?"

"Wise King," Xymod said.

And then he then began to tell the story of the legend, the impending doom of the Zarnegy, and of their quest to recover the Shards and save the galaxy. The companions did note he didn't mention the Amulet. The king and Auffi listened intently to Xymod's story, with all the respect it obviously deserved. After Xymod had finished, there was a long silence as it was obvious that the king was going to choose his words wisely.

"I dunno what you lot have been smoking. It's obviously some kindah wacky weed if you think you can waltz on in as if it's to'wist season, info'wming me you want my most sac'wed jewel. The'we is no F-intheway you f'weeloadah's a'we getting your hands anywhe'we near my family's p'wized possession and hei'wloom. The only way you will evah get this gem would be if you p'wized it f'wom my cold, dead hands," the king shouted at the companions.

That could certainly be arranged, Nickolas thought.

Xymod looked at the Shard, still sitting in its usual place. "Why is this Shard so valuable to you? It doesn't wield any power for you or help your people in any way. If you let us have it, you will be rewarded beyond your wildest dreams."

"But you have al'weady re'wa'wded me," the king replied, "with info'wmation. Now you have confi'wmed it has unlimited po'wah, which I am now dete'wmined to mastah. I might have a go at ruling the galaxy myself. I mean, it's not as though collecting taxes, while babbling on about the latest banana c'wop repo'wt f'wom Pe'wtion 26, is hard wo'wk for those dodgy senatah's on Ge'wtion 1, is it?"

"I think you would do fine on Gertion 1. You would be right at home with all the other galaxies' biggest plonkers," Nickolas said to no one in particular, however it did look as though the king overheard him.

"Gua'wds!" the king cried, and immediately his private guard came from out of nowhere and surrounded the party. "I have hea'wd enough. Please th'wow our 'valued visitahs' into the dungeons below. Maybe they will lea'wn some respect."

"You will regret this decision. It's an ill wind that blows no one some good King," Xymod said with a strange resolve in his voice. "You are a blind, stupid fool if you think you will ever gain control of the Shard. It has a mind of its own and cannot be controlled."

"How da'we you! I have NEVAH been so insulted so much in all my life!" the king bellowed.

"Then you should get out more," Nickolas said, attempting to calm proceedings down in his usual, mild-mannered way.

"And jailah. Feel f'wee to th'wow away the key."

"We will be back later this night-cycle to collect you," Xymod communicated to the Shard, as the companions were being led out of the king's chamber, towards the dungeon below.

"I will be ready," Vigor replied.

"Told you we should have gone with my plan, mates," Techno chirped in, as the guards went about disarming them. They were then roughly shoved into one big holding cell.

"I hate to admit it, however, for once, I think our little green friend is right. I think it was a mistake to tell the king the truth and appeal to his good nature. Even if we do find a way to escape, the throne room will surely be more jolly well-guarded than the liquor cabinet at an Alcoholics Anonymous meeting," Jonathan said in rather a frustrated tone.

"Serenity now, Jonathan. We will have the Shard in good time. *Patience is a virtue,*" Xymod said.

"More like 'insanity now' to be closely followed by 'total stupidity later'," Nickolas said, as he took up residency on one of the solid rock pews in their cell. "I hope the dungeon food is palatable. I would hate to be tortured to death on an empty stomach."

13. The Pretubo Sisters

"BECAUSE 'PREPARIN ONE'S OWN MEAL WUZ SO LAST SUN-CYCLE'."

The Pretubo sisters were known throughout the galaxy as the team you could rely on to transform someone from being alive and kicking, to being so dead the mourners would often be tempted to bury them twice. They were hired mercenaries, killers of the highest order, and it was almost an honour to be on their hit list as it showed someone out there cared enough to invest more than a pretty penny to see you six feet under.

It's fair to say these chicks didn't need much encouragement to rock and roll. A point not lost on Thomas, who spent a lot of time clarifying clearly to Victus and Rictus Pretubo, the scope of their assignment.

"To confirm … again," Thomas said, as the sisters were enjoying an exotic meal of what remarkably resembled bangers and mash. These bangers and mash, mind you, were randomly teleported from some other part of the galaxy, because 'preparin one's own meal wuz so last sun-cycle' the sisters informed Thomas.

"Your assignment is to assist me in locating and capturing the Milarum brothers. I need them alive as they have important information as to the whereabouts of the Amulet and Shards we're looking for. Now, as they might or might not have this on their person, I don't want you two blowing them away until I have that information, okay?"

"Capture, not kill. Okay, dis be some new concept fo' us. However, whut da damn hell. Let's suck it and see, shall we?"

Victus said in a tone that suggested she was doing the galaxy a favour.

"Okay, let me spell this out for you another way. If I see dead people, you two see no credits. Clear?"

"Territo," Rictus said.

"We do get t' maim still though, right?" Victus enquired.

"If you must," Thomas said, shaking his head in bemusement.

The Pretubo sisters and Thomas reached Aertion 12 at around the same time the Milarum's arrived at the Realm of the Gas Giants. Wasting no time, they headed directly to the central security centre of the Cutthroat Casino and viewed pretty much the same footage the QLEB officers had viewed a short time before. From there they continued in to the recently vacated Milarum room, to further investigate.

They searched the room and found only a note, which read:
Word Up and Peace Out Folks! #Sorryaboutthemess.
Salutations, Muck-a-muck Milarum.

"What do you two know about these Gas Giants?" Thomas asked.

"Sweet funk all," Rictus replied. "Then again, ya' didn't brin us along fo' our knowledge of de local inhabitants o' even our ace good looks, fo' dat matter."[68]

"Howeva', we do know one thin though," Rictus said with an awfully predictable tone in her voice.

"Go on." Thomas knew exactly which direction this conversation was marching in, which wasn't hard, as every conversation with these two tended to involve some reference to the topic of non-stop violence. He decided to play along anyway.

---

[68] Which was a relief because both were athletic in appearance, but they had the facial features even their mother found hard to stomach.

"That if their surname ain't Milarum, dey are in deep, deep trouble," Rictus said, with a huge grin on her hideous face.

"I do need to team up with less violent companions moving forward," Thomas said to no one in particular as they headed down the hotel corridor, enroute back to his ship. "Maybe the Suicide-bomb-Kevenings of the 'Killiniskewl' cult on Nertion 213 would be more balanced individuals than you two."

"Probably. But we wiped dem Suicide-bomb-Kevenings out recently fo' some laughs in-between jobs. So, I guess ya' will neva' know," Victus said with a gummy smile.

14. Master Jailer Jillicia

"I BET HE IS PISSING IN HIS PANTS NOW."

Gwendolyn and Romeo reached the Realm of the Gas Giants around mid-sun-cycle. They landed their ship close enough to the capital's front gates so as not to give the wrong impression, but far enough away that if should they have to retreat hastily, which often was necessary in their experience, they would be able to do so. They announced their credentials at the gates and requested an audience with the king on urgent QLEB business.

"Oh, the joy," remarked King Geffkl, on learning that yet another party of foreigners had arrived and demanded an audience. "We haven't had this many pesky outsidah visitahs in eons. Then suddenly we get two g'woups, in the same cycle? Both demanding to see me immediately? Co-ink-ee-dink?"

"I doubt it, my excellence. Possibly our to'wism depa'wtment is running a campaign?" Auffi said.

"We have a to'wism depa'wtment? Remind me to visit this head of to'wism a little latah then, and cong'watulate him pe'wsonally with about twelve rounds f'wom my ConVosa pistol."

"No p'woblem, sir. I will pencil him in, so you can rub him out."

By the time the QLEB officers had been escorted to the throne room, Auffi and King Geffkl had more than ample time to get even more ticked off, especially after they lost a bundle of credits on a slug race, which had recently finished on Omertian 6. Apparently, a hot tip had been found in one of the prisoner's pockets.

When Gwendolyn and Romeo were finally graced with an

audience, the king simply shouted, "Gua'wds! You know the d'will. Lock them up."

Romeo was obviously taken aback by this turn of events. "You-do-realise-we-are-officers-of-the-Qurkition-Law-Enforcement-Bureau?-BEEP-BEEP-You-can't-lock-us-up!-BEEP-BEEP-I-mean-you-er-we-haven't-even-asked-any-questions?-BEEP-BEEP"

"Watch me, you pileah metal t'wash," the king replied, as he continued on with what he was doing. He didn't even look up. "Your pointless QLEB laws have no meaning he'we. If you feel ha'wd done by, please feel f'wee to fill out a complaint t'wansmission at your ea'wliest convenience. In the meantime, make you'wselves at home, in one of my many p'wemium to'wist apa'wtments."

"You vill rrregrrret tis, King," Gwendolyn shouted as they were escorted away.

"I totally ag'wee," the king replied. "This enti'we sun-cycle has been one big fat 'rrregrrret' so far. But thanks for ca'wing. I app'weciate it." Moments later Romeo and Gwendolyn were introduced to the Gas Giants' premium tourist apartments, the dungeon holding facilities.

Jillicia, the master jailer, was having the time of his life. A natural born bully, he was tormenting and intimidating older Gas Giant toddlers before he could walk. It was obvious even then that Jillicia was destined for a career in corrections. So, when the previous master jailer went bat-shit crazy[69], Jillicia was appointed to the position. It was like a dream come true.

"I am being paid for doing my one and only love," he often spouted to anyone who would listen. The only glitch with his

---

[69] Apparently, he was so bored one sun-cycle that he snapped and ended up locking himself in a cell and throwing away the key.

dream job was that no sane person ever dared venture into Gas Giant territory. And as the Gas Giants never locked up any of their own, it meant he rarely had any 'guests' in his facilities.

Who could blame potential visitors anyway? The Gas Giants realm was situated on a wasteland on the western coastline of the smallest continent on Aertion 12 and away from pretty much everything of interest.[70] This lead most of the planet's tourism companies[71] to say that visiting the Gas Giants Realm was about as interesting as hiring a Watcher-Bug from Bertion 3.[72]

So, after several solar-cycles of locking up sweet bugger all, Jillicia now had not only multiple prisoners in his dungeon, but more were on the way. He could now unleash his full repertoire of new bullying techniques on someone other than his poor, long suffering wife, who tolerated him and his regular bully simulation workshops only because they were fully catered.

Jillicia slammed the cell door on his newest arrivals and hurried back to his office, eager to figure out which of his prisoners he was going to put to the proverbial sword first. He did have the common dungeon-house decency to stop outside the first cell on his way back to his office and pull out the old 'point three of his fingers at all three of his eyes, then point the same three fingers at one of his captives,' in this case, it was Techno. It was a cheap shot.

Obviously not conversant in Gas Giant dungeoneer bullying

---

[70] Unless you enjoy the smell of stinking gas and the company of real giants.

[71] Everyone except The Aertion 12 Stinking Gas Touring Company. Although the last anyone had heard of them, they were thinking of changing their name. And their tours. And the planet they were touring on.

[72] A Watcher-Bug from Bertion 3 was the bug you hired if you wanted someone to watch you do nothing for five full sun-cycles straight, then provide a three-thousand-page report afterwards. Thrown in for good measure was a full ten-cycle debriefing of its observations. It was riveting stuff. It was all the rage with the super-vain crowd on the sloth planet of Dertion 54.

techniques, Techno looked over his shoulder, as if Jillicia was pointing at something interesting on the dungeon wall behind him.

I bet he is pissing in his pants now, Jillicia thought as he continued wandering and whistling down the corridor.

"So, QLEB officer Gwendolyn Wang," came a casual voice from the darkness, at the back of the adjacent cell. "Of all the cells, in all the galaxy, you had to wind up next to mine. What did they lock you up for? You two haven't opened one of your greasy spoons on this planet here, have you? If that is the case, it's about time you two gastro-criminals were arrested."

"Oh, dearrrie me," Gwendolyn said without looking up. "If it isn't the 'infamous' Nickolas Milarrrum. I smelt a strrrong odourrr of loserrr as soon as I landed on ze planet. Do I spot anotherrr infamous face also?" she said as she caught a glimpse of something green sitting in the corner next to Nickolas. "Hov arrre you, Prrrince Techno? Altough morrre disturrrbingly, vhy arrre you still sitting in tat cell? I mean, it's a prrretty basic design frrrom vhat I have seen, especially considerrring ze ones you have escaped frrrom overrr ze cycles. Most of vhich I have put you in myself, I might add."

"Oh! G'cycle Gwendolyn," Techno said casually. "Yeah, I know. But it has been requested by Jonathan I stay bloody put." He moved into better light so Gwendolyn and Romeo could see he had both hands tied behind his back.

"Sound carrreerrr advice, my little grrreen frrriend. I vill have to rrrememberrr tat next time I have you locked up."

"Now, now, children. Behave," Nerada said. She also stood and moved into better light, closer to the central bars which separated the two cells.

"That's no way to talk to a prince," Nerada said, glancing at

Techno, who looked about as regal as the lavatory maintenance crew on the last cycle of a thirty-six sun-cycle gig by the biggest thrash metal band in the galaxy, ☗⌐✗⬛⊖ℛ⬛ℐ⌐✓☐⚔✓✗[73].

"Who are you two anyway?" Nerada said as she sized up the two QLEB officers, "and how come 'we' apparently know you?"

"Other than being, without a doubt, the worst two restaurateurs in the galaxy," Nickolas interrupted, "they are probably the two best QLEB officers on the force. So, taking a wild stab in the dark here, I get the feeling they're here to question us, for some strange reason."

"Milarrrum! It appearrrs yourrr brrrain vorrrks afterrrall. It must be ze foul gas in ze airrr, powerrring it along," Gwendolyn said. "Yes, ve have been looking forrr you lot. And consequently, ve have some questions to put to you. Fill in ze blank-type questions, so to speak."

"Jolly good show," Jonathan said, moving forward. "We're happy to answer your questions, officers. I mean it's not as though we have anything to hide."

"Glad-to-hear-BEEP-BEEP." Added Romeo

"Speak for yourself, brother," Nickolas said, as he smirked at Gwendolyn.

"Let's-then-let's-start-with-an-easy-one-BEEP-BEEP," Romeo said in a stern, electronic voice. "Can-you-explain-what-you-were-doing-trolling-through-the-CRAP-database-looking-for-information-on-ancient-legends-BEEP-BEEP?"

"Well, my old trash-compactor chum," Nickolas said, "we truly wish we were in a position where we could even confirm,

---

[73] You might have heard of them, with popular tracks including: 'All things perish … but not before my ex does', and my personal favourite, 'Die, bean counter, die, but please finish my tax return first'.

or deny, that line of inquiry. However, if we did do such a thing, which we didn't, we wouldn't be able to tell you anyway, because, frankly, that information, if it did come to light, which of course it won't, because, ipso facto, we didn't do it, would be above your pay grade anyway. I hope this clears the matter up," he concluded, in the smuggest tone probably ever muttered in Qurkition history. Even smugger than Eopo Mobo of Dertion 67.[74]

"Sorrrry," Gwendolyn said unapologetically. "I tuned out at trrrash-compactorrr. I vould apprrreciate it if someone oterrr tan Nickolas would take a crrrack at lying strrraight to ourrr faces."

Techno winked at Nickolas. "Sure thing, mate." He stood up, cleared his throat, and was about to pull out another one of his highly entertaining stories[75] when Jonathan stepped forward and put a hand over Techno's mouth.

"Enough, by jove. The truth of the matter, in short form, is the legend of Octarm is true. Our companion, Xymod here, is in fact a legendary Collector of the Octarma, and we are here to seek a Shard. The ancient Shard of Vigor, the first of three we intend to place in the Amulet. We are doing this so we can help save the galaxy against the threat of the Black Mist and the evil Zarnegy."

Gwendolyn gave each of the inmates in the adjacent cell a

---

[74] On winning the equivalent of his planet's lottery, the Voimiopoloisfh, (try pronouncing that after a few cocktails) Eopo Mobo seized control of the architectural firm he worked for via a hostile takeover. He then systematically sacked every member of staff who had ever taken issue or criticised his 'revolutionary' work on rooftops. "It's time to turn this company around, and I am the top man for the job," he was often cited boasting at company functions. He, of course, wasn't the top man for the job for two simple reasons:

    1: The firm didn't need turning around. It was already super-successful, and

    2: He was a talentless hack, and only kept his job because he was married to the owner's daughter.

[75] Probably the one about the night-cycle he acquired (stole) a revolutionary experimental particle shrinking cannon after one too many drinks at a late-night-cycle bar on Dertion 301, and where the now missing planet of Dertion 302, went to.

good, hard look. "I can't believe I am saying tis. Howeverrr, I tink I believe terrre is morrre trrrut in Nickolas's ansverrr, as you arrre all clearrrly having a laugh."

"My dear young lady," Xymod said, stepping forward and staring her right in the eyes, "perhaps this demonstration will change your perspective. *Doubt is the deadliest enemy of any dream*"

Xymod reached inside his coat and whispered the word *"Apparente."* Magically, the Octarm Amulet, that he had hidden with a spell when they were captured, reappeared. As if on cue, the tiny jewels that surrounded the empty slots on the Amulet started to spark, then lit up and spun at an astonishing rate, which held each of the inmates in some sort of spell.

While under the trance, everyone could have sworn the Amulet spoke to them. It displayed the history of the Qurkition galaxy and the origin of its people and planets. It told them of the common thread that bound them together, and also of the destructive force of the Black Mist and the Zarnegy.

Only that Nerada saw a different vision — a vision of a distant galaxy. A galaxy full of planets, which looked dormant, but that were slowly beginning to return to life. Each of these planets was surrounded by a faint reddish glow. These planets were full of inhabitants, who looked identical to her.

A few moments later, although it felt longer, the jewels stopped spinning and each companion's trance ended. After this show of power, everyone was quiet for some time, each contemplating what they had just seen.

"As much as I vant to believe yourrr trrrue intentions herrre, hoveverrr honourrrable, ve arrre still underrr orrrderrrs to brrring you in forrr questioning. I prrromise we vill furrrtherrr investigate yourrr storrry, once ve have you all back at headquarrrterrrs," Gwendolyn said.

"I do enjoy your enthusiasm on the subject of locking us up again," Nickolas said. "But I would consider, in our current predicament, that we all welcome ourselves to the 'cotton-on club' and have Techno here break us out of this joint."

"You cerrrtainly have a vay vith vorrrds, Milarrrum. Shame tose vorrrds arrre rrrarrrely in any vay coherrrent."

A strange voice chimed in from the poorly lit back corner of the Milarum's cell, "We could take that plan of action, however, I for one am happy to wait it out until this night-cycle. The Gas Giants are an active, dangerous lot by sun-cycle. However, in a few cycles after dark, they all pass out. I slipped something into their gas stream some time ago, so they stopped causing too much trouble for the other inhabitants of the planet. Then once the coast is clear, let's be on our way." Xyrapt stepped into the light, and casually sat next to Nickolas and Techno.

"How the hell did you get in here?" Nerada asked, genuinely startled.

"Yeah," Nickolas said, "who, in the buggery are you, and why would you break *into* a dungeon cell?"

"I am Xyrapt Patronus, at your service." He offered Nickolas a half nod and high-fived Techno. "Given this is my planet," he continued as he stood, and walked through the wall into the next dungeon cell, shook Gwendolyn's hand, and nodded to Romeo[76].

"I tend to drift around as I please." He returned to the Milarum's cell and stood next to Xymod.

"Oh, *that* Xyrapt. The same Xyrapt who sent us to this stinking cesspit in the first place. Thanks for taking the time to

---

[76] The QLEB officers couldn't have looked more surprised if the Great Qurkition restaurant menu judges had rolled up to one of their restaurants and awarded it four Reebin Stars — (think Michelin, only better).

stop by. Do feel free to teach me the walking through solid walls trick some-cycle," Nickolas said casually, as the rest of the party looked at Xyrapt in utter amazement. "Jonathan and I could do with an encore for our act."

"Why?" Nerada asked as she started to untie Techno's hands. "It's not as though you ever had a call to perform an encore in the first place."

15. The Fiddle Stick Theory

"WHO IS FLYING THAT SHIP? A BLIND FOO-BAT FROM BE'WTION 7?"

Thomas and the Pretubo sisters made their grand arrival in the Gas Giant's capital around mid-late-sun-cycle. They achieved this feat by landing uninvited, smack-bang in the middle of one of the biggest courtyards in the city. They then demanded to see the king immediately, regarding his Shard.

As you can imagine, on hearing that a third party of outsiders had, not only destroyed his favourite courtyard, but also had designs on his beloved Shard, the king had what could only be described as a visHamogus hissy fit[77].

When King Geffkl finally calmed down, he told this latest set of unwanted guests, in no uncertain terms, that tourism season had officially ended with the sudden death of the Tourism Minister and the devolving of the Gas Giant Tourism Department. This was confirmed when Auffi showed them a live feed of the dungeon cells as proof of the fact that their visitor quarters where now full. Of course, the Milarum brothers were immediately recognised by Thomas.

"Now push off and annoy some othah poor sap somewhe'we else befo'we something unfo'wtunate happens to you all," the king said. "Oh, and Auffi, any fu'wthah requests conce'wning my Sha'wd or any other b'wight ideas, should be put into a communication and t'wansmitted to someone who ca'wes."

---

[77] Aptly named for the moment in-between Eloise visHamogus's usually highly animated reaction to anytime her credit is declined, and the point she pulls out her ConVoser.

The visHamogus party's reply wasn't what King Geefkl was expecting.

"It's painfully simple, whutever ya' name be, ya' better hand over de Shard we require, sharpish, or, ya' will have me layin ya', alon with some ov these stinkin, gigantic freaks ya' call subjects, on cement planks." Victus shouted.

"Why thank you," the king, who was now beyond bursting point, replied, "for your wo'wds of wisdom. I will take it undah advisement. Please do note, the only reason you a'wen't joining my fo'wmah To'wism Ministah in pe'wmanent 'Incompetent Utopia'[78] right now is because killin' an outsidah on fi'wst contact is conside'wed bad luck in our cultu'we. So think you'wself lucky."

"Oh, *please* do go on, ya' grand majestic holiness," Rictus said ominously, as she leaned forward and silently unclipped her ConVoser pistol holster, while glancing over and nodding to her sister.

"I would st'wongly suggest you lot c'wawl back undah whatevah aste'woid you came f'wom. Because if I EVAH have the displeasu'we of c'wossing your paths again, I will shoot you, repeatedly. Only stopping aftah your co'wpses have tu'wned cold or mushy." By this time the King Geffkl was foaming from the mouth with rage.

"Take dis under advisement ... dirt bag," Rictus said as she pulled out her weapon. But before she could 'advise' the king eight times with her ConVoser-4, Thomas leapt in and wrenched the gun from her hand. Regrettably, he didn't notice her sister had also unholstered her pistol, and before he could stop her, she had already advised the king of twelve bursts.

---

[78] And yes, there is such a promised land. Where else do you think middle management executives go when they die?

You would think job done; the king is history. However, if they had bothered to do any research on the Gas Giants, they would have found out one of the reasons they have gas in their name was because a gas-type substance formed a field of protection around the Giant, completely protecting them from small, light arm weapon fire.

Thomas and his party were now in a spot of trouble. All of the court's guards had activated their own personal gas-shields and pulled out their weapons with every intention of blowing these outsiders clean back into the last millennium.

"Hold your fi'we!" the king shouted, as Thomas and the sisters threw their weapons down and put their hands up. "Let them go!" he continued, with a strange grin on his face.

"What, what, what!" Auffi shouted, ready to paint the palace floor a nice, new colour called 'visHamogus-and-friends-red.'

"As our ancient p'wophesy states: Our families will get th'wee solar-cycles of bad luck if we shoot you now. Howevah if I let you go, the next time I see you, it will be for the second time. And if my math is co'wect, I would say it would be the last time I see you also."

Thomas's party didn't need a second invitation to make an exit. But Thomas had to drag the sisters out by their ponytails, which amused the Gas Giants no end, especially when Thomas had to use all his strength to keep the sisters from breaking free of his grasp. This evoked much finger pointing and mocking laughter.

"Gua'wds, p'wepa'we my ship for immediate depa'wtu'we," the king, said, through maniacal laughter.

As soon as Thomas and the Pretubo twins were free of the palace, Thomas contacted Sam1atha and informed her to heat up those engines, as they were coming in red-hot.

His next call was to his father. "We might have to go with Plan B, Father. The Gas Giants will not give up the Shard the Milarum's, who are currently locked in their dungeon."

"Lucky then that I've already taken the liberty of activating Plan B."

"Why am I not surprised?" Thomas shook his head. "I hope Plan B doesn't involve either myself or our overly excitable friends here. We're a little tied up at the moment, running for our lives, with half a nation of Gas Giants in pursuit."

"Oh, I wouldn't worry about them. Set your course for the coordinates that I've transferred to your personal communicator. You'll be fine, sonny boy."

Thomas had by now managed to drag the sisters, kicking and screaming the entire way, back to the ship. He relayed in the directions received from his father to Sama1tha.

"Sama1tha, please head to these coordinates. Let's punch it now, if you please. I get the distinct impression our welcome here is about as worn out as my sisters' favourite drinking glass, and that we're about to become target practice."

The king and most of his personal guards had already boarded the king's royal space-cruiser. He was looking forward to a leisurely late-cycle of hunting, destroying, and killing Thomas and his nasty little companions, and anything else that took his fancy. "Oh, I am one lucky Giant sometimes," the king beamed.

"It ce'wtainly is a nice pe'wk, mixing one's favo'wite hobby with wo'wk." He took up position on his royal lounge, located in the centre of his ship's main bridge, and ordered a chilled

Swiby[79] from the bar.

"Have fun, my holiness. You haven't had any pe'wsonal time in ages," Auffi stated, who reluctantly stayed behind to attend to Gasstro matters.

"Thanks, my loyal se'wvant. Once I have finished this bunch off, Could you please info'wm the masta jailah to p'wepa'we our othah guests for depa'wtchah also." The king smiled wickedly. "Pe'wmanent depa'wtchah."

"With pleasure, your eminence," came the reply from Auffi, who also had a wide grin on his face as he ended transmission.

The Gas Giant King's hunt commenced in a grand manner. Thomas' ship launched, turned 180 degrees, and roared straight past the king's ship. This made it easy for the Gas Giants' cruiser to pick up their trail and follow it as it headed into orbit.

"Who is flying that ship? A blind foo-bat from Be'wtion 7?" the king asked, as the made absolutely no attempt to escape, or even change course.

"Don't fo'wget to blast their hyper-d'wive. We don't want our fun to get any b'wight ideas of escape now, do we?" the king commanded his gun crew.

The king's ship fired and strategically damaged two of the four primary engine power-units and the vortex-drive on Thomas' ship. That's what Sama1tha told the Gas Giants' ships damage report computer anyway. The entire Gas Giant crew laughed.

"To'wist season could be a good thing aftah all." The king laughed as his ship continued to fire liberally at the *Aletheia*.

The smile was wiped from his face when a few moments

---

[79] A swiby is a small, arachnid-like creature whose bite turns your insides the colour of a concoction of ice-cold red wine, some kind of fizzy sparkly water with red, fruity ice cream. A swiby is very nice to drink on a hot sun-cycle.

later their short-range scanners started to pick up a huge number of incoming ships. These craft were flying right into their trajected flight path. By the time the king put 'visHamogus and fleet' together, it was too late.

To his credit, the king, in one last brave act of defiance, launched everything in his ship's arsenal at the visHamogus fleet. He then immediately surrendered, citing galactic law GL— 2765—7613—13.2, which clearly states: 'If you're in a no-win situation, try and surrender. You never know, the suckers might go for it.' It was obvious from the prompt reply received moments later that the visHamogus fleet had no legal representation present.[80]

The king, however, did manage to utter what would be his last words, "Oh, fiddle sticks!" before his ship was destroyed. These last words went viral on every communication medium in the galaxy. Even the extremely unpopular dating site, Palm-FACE.[81]

Later, 12th Squadron Leader, Suicide Psyche, claimed the kill, even though the king's ship was hit with so much firepower, from almost every craft in the visHamogus armada, that his vessel wasn't only completely incinerated, it was virtually erased from the history books all together.

"Don't you love Plan B," Thomas said to the Pretubo sisters, as Sam1atha swung the *Aletheia* around, and took up the lead position at the head of the visHamogus fleet.

"Time to put a further little ripple in the Gas Giant's cycle."

The visHamogus invading fleet entered the local

---

[80] Who can blame them? Considering the ludicrous retainers charged by a good intergalactic criminal lawyer.

[81] The last thing that Thomas visHamogus heard about this was Palm-FACE were talking production rights for 'Oh Fiddle Sticks: The last pointless but heroic stand of Geffkl Deennu, Gas Giant King'.

atmosphere of Aertion 12 with a deafening roar. So deafening, that even the hard of hearing on the neighbouring planet Aertion 13 considered putting in a noise complaint to their local law enforcement agency.

Sadly, noise pollution was the least of the Gas Giants' problems. Before they knew what hit them, the visHamogus long-range cruisers launched missile attacks on the city, destroying key infrastructure and decimating entire suburbs of Gasstro and their population within moments.

To make matters worse, small short-range fighters also launched from the fleet's escort cruisers to carry out low range bombing runs and destroying other parts of the city. What was left of the Gas Giants' military command had gathered in the throne room to argue about their next course of action.

Auffi, his head bowed in grief since the news of his beloved king's demise, listened in silence as the Gas Giant's military command gave the distinct impression that they would find it challenging to organise an escape from a wet paper bag, let alone formulate a competent plan to defend the capital city.

After a few moments, Auffi, tears still streaming down his face, stood and approached the control panel on the king's throne. He pressed the large red button marked: 'Let's hope we never need to press this big red button.'

The sound of something very large could be heard powering itself up throughout the city. Auffi then picked up his War-Pole, turned to the rest of the Giants present and bellowed, "Kill them. Kill them all!"

"The Gas Giants have activated some sort of defensive shield, sir. It's covering the entire city," General Voolok, the commander of the visHamogus invasion fleet, said via his inter-ship communicator. "Our weapons are unable to penetrate it.

Nevertheless, we will increase the power ratio and keep trying."

"I doubt you will have any luck, General," Thomas said. "My ship's computer has informed me it's some sort of nuclear-based gas-shield, totally capable of repelling anything we can hit it with. We have no choice other than to land and deploy our ground troops. It seems we'll have to do this the hard way."

"Yes, sir. We will attack the city walls directly."

Within moments, an assault troop transport ship launched from the visHamogus troopship carrier landed outside the range of the force field and the city's defensive weapons. Thousands of heavily armed troops disembarked and formed ranks.

The *Aletheia* returned to the planet's surface and landed closer to the city's gates than the rest of the troops. Saman1tha cloaked the before it could draw any unwanted attention from the city's defensive gun turrets.

"I damn got da need. De need t' damn succeed," Rictus announced, as she inserted even more weapons into her commando belt, recalibrating them as she went to bypass the Giants personal shields.

"Time t' kick de tyres and light da damn fires," Victus said, doing the same.

Thomas blocked their exit. "Oh, no you don't. I'm going with you."

"Ya' do what ya' need t' do, visHamogus. But ya' had better keep up, cuz we plan on doin some runnin, stunnin, and gunnin," Victus said.

The sisters sidestepped Thomas and leapt from the open airlock onto the planet's surface.

"I still want the Milarum's alive," Thomas shouted, following them as quickly as he could.

"Ya' are probably da only one who does. As I can't imagine

da damn Gas Giants are goin t' be overly homey now dat their king's dead and their beloved city bein blown t' dust," Victus shouted as both the sisters broke into a run.

"That may be. Nonetheless, stay close, and we will see if we can break through to the king's palace," Thomas said, struggling to keep up.

The sisters, who had obviously read from the same tactical combat book as Prince Techno, ran straight at the front gates, all ConVoser-4 hand weapons blazing. As they neared, Rictus pulled out a grenade and in one smooth motion activated the device and slung-shot it with great precision so that it landed at the base of the left gate.

Moments later, the little device exploded, taking half the reinforced gate with it. Without breaking stride, the Pretubo sisters ran through the breach and did what they do best.

The Gas Giants' defence of the city was looking grim. This was made worse thanks to the city's insurance company, YoYO (You're on Your Own) Inc.[82], informing them, via massive screens spread throughout the city, that any damage caused by this invasion, or any subsequent invasion, would not be covered in their policy. This was as per section 78.1.4.3.7.23 and located under the heading 'Bad Karma for Bad People,' which clearly

---

[82] The insurance company in question, YoYO (You're on Your Own) Inc., prided itself on never once approving a claim in its illustrious 362-solar-cycle history. During their inductions, new recruits are told the horror story of Mr Comm Fvmy of Pertion 154. Comm, who spent his entire life studying the 455,000 page YoYO Insurance Ts & Cs document, figured out a successful claim could be processed if he broke his leg while waiting for an inter-city public transport vehicle, on a particular corner of a particular suburb, so long as it happened on an exact date, at an exact time, and on the eighth leap lunar-cycle of the century.
Fortunately for corporation's galaxy-wide, YoYO was saved as poor Comm perished while executing his not so cunningly conceived plan. He miscalculated his leg-to-curb ratio and ended up being fatally run down by the transport vehicle he was waiting so patiently to be badly injured by. So much for tackling corporate greed on your own.

stated: 'that any destruction caused to themselves, or their property (including emotional) was not covered.'

Thomas was too busy trying to keep up with the Pretubo sisters to glance up at the monitors showing some YoYO employee, dressed in extremely expensive attire, playing on a loop and saying, "Sorry. Claim Denied. But given you lot are mostly an unpleasant race anyway, bad karma was bound to catch up to you some-cycle, so live with it."

"Keep up, visHamogus, o' I'm goin to shoot ya' myself," Victus shouted, as she disarmed, then shot an attacking Gas Giant guard at close range, all in one fluid motion.

Thomas, now running at full speed, could only watch with mild admiration as the sisters continued on their merry way heading straight towards the palace. Any Gas Giant silly enough to cross their paths certainly wished a few moments later, after a quick scan to count how many appendages they had left, that they'd kept their brave acts of 'For King and Country' firmly to themselves. By now, the Gas Giants defiance, which was always half-hearted at best, started to crumble completely, as visHamogus ground troops entered the city via the breach in the gate. As far as the average Gas Giant was concerned, if these invading buffoons wanted this gas filled hellhole, they called Gasstro so badly, it was all theirs, and good luck to them.

16. The Black Mist

"ALL HAIL, KING TECHNO, RULER OF WHAT'S LEFT
OF THIS CRUMMY REALM."

The Gas Giant's dungeons were deep underground. Far enough down that the Milarum party and the QLEB officers wouldn't have heard much of the commotion that was transpiring on the planet's surface, even if they were awake, which they weren't, courtesy of the sleeping gas that Master Jailer Jillicia had pumped into their cells.

The companions were all awoken by something else — something way more sinister than the invading visHamogus fleet.

"What is this stuff?" Nerada asked, as she found their cell engulfed in some sort of thick, black vapour, which soaked into everything, making it extremely hard to breathe.

"To me, quickly," Xymod ordered. He put one hand on the Amulet, casting a protective shield around the companions, who had gathered around him.

"What the hell is going on?" Nickolas said.

"It's the Black Mist," Xymod replied. "They have found us, and the Shard."

"So, folks. Given these latest developments, I can safely confirm it's time to make our jolly well way out of here," Jonathan said. He had picked his words carefully, hoping to sound as intelligent as possible.

"How lovely it is of you to share your little plan with us," Nickolas retorted. "Next time when I'm appearing on Qurkition Challenge, and I need a subject matter expert on 'the flipping obvious' remind me to look you up."

A moment later, Xyrapt appeared from nowhere. "They are here, Xymod. And I don't mean the visHamogus' invading fleet."

"Yes, I know. The disciples of Victarm are upon us. *Out of the frying pan, into the fire.*"

"The visHamogus are here and attacking also?" Nerada asked.

"Yes," Xyrapt said.

"Obviously here for the Amulet and Shard too," Jonathan remarked. "Felicity was right."

"Either way, they are of no significance compared to the Zarnegy," Xyrapt said. "There is no time to lose."

He waved his hand and the doors to the cells holding the Milarum's and the QLEB officers swung open. "Hurry, or all is lost."

Once outside the cells, the companions dashed to the jailer's office to reclaim their possessions. They found Jillicia locked in a heated discussion — he didn't appear to have noticed his city was being systematically blown to bits — with Jonathan's iNegotiat device, which had taken it upon itself to try and negotiate for the companions' release.

iNegotiat: Look, you fat, ugly moron. They may be losers, but please let them loose. I mean, take a gander at their stupid faces. They didn't do anything; they are way too stupid. You can't lock people up for being stupid, can you?"

Jillicia: Oh, yah they did. They insulted dah king.

iNegotiat: No they didn't.

Jillicia: Oh, yah they did.

iNegotiat: Oh, no they didn't.

Jillicia: Oh, yah they did.

iNegotiat: Oh, no they didn't.

It was only when Techno knocked on the half open door and asked for directions to the penitentiary gift shop that Jillicia re-entered the world of reality. "Why, you little!" he cried, as he took a lunge at Techno, which the prince easily evaded.

The party quickly descended on Jillicia, with about the same brute force as a tonne of nitroglycerine, Especially Gwendolyn, who after asking for more seasoning in the poor excuse for a luncheon they were served earlier, was disappointed Jillicia had brought ground black pepper, instead of the socially acceptable cracked variety in a grinder.

"I mean it is not rrrocket science," she had commented to Romeo. Everyone knew cracked pepper worked better with dungeon gruel.

After the companions had tied Jillicia to his chair, they re-acquainted themselves with their equipment, which had been confiscated on their imprisonment.

"You can't leave!" Jillicia shouted in defiance. "My execution plan will be ruined." Desperation radiated from his eyes.

"Sorry for putting you out," Nickolas said. "Think of this as the monster of all bad management er … variations."

The companions started leaving Jillicia's quarters, enroute to the throne room.

"Good work, old boy," Jonathan said, as he picked up the iNegotiat and gave it a little kiss.

"Thanks. Glad to help. I had him on the proverbial ropes there. Pity he was a moron," iNegotiat replied, in its usual cheery tone.

Techno was the last to leave the office, but not before taking time out of his busy schedule to rifle through Jillicia's office drawers and pockets for anything useful. For Techno, this was pretty much everything which wasn't nailed down. He also took great pleasure in returning the finger and eye pointing exercise to Jillicia, except with two fingers and two eyes.

When all the companions had left the room, Jillicia broke down and started sobbing. He had never been bullied before, especially by someone smaller than him and boy, did it truly hurt.

The companions were soon clear of the dungeon and climbing their way up the stairs to the palace above. Jonathan used his recently re-acquired communicator to contact his sister.

"So, as you can imagine, old girl, I don't think the Zarnegy the visHamogus are here for the jolly reasonable real estate prices," Jonathan concluded.

"What did I tell you?" Felicity said. "I knew Thomas and his sister were up to no good. That family is about as predictable as Zel Zal."[83]

"What did you ruddy expect?" Jonathan said. "Thomas didn't get the nickname 'trust-me-not-Tommy' in school for nothing."

"You're okay though, right?" Felicity asked in an unusually concerned tone.

"Yes, we are ALL fine," Nerada butted in. "Thanks for taking an interest. Oh, which also includes two QLEB agents

---

[83] Zel Zal, from Gertion 38, was famous for every solar-cycle travelling all the way to Aertion 12 to play the famous Ccoolo Wheel for his chance to win his dream super-craft, The Annihilator. For ten solar-cycles straight, he would save every spare credit he had, visit Aertion 12 and bet his entire fortune on his favourite number: twonineone. It's a damn shame that Zel never learnt to understand or read numbers properly — he felt it held him back career wise, as an accountant — because he would have discovered long ago the Ccoolo Wheel numbering system only ran from twenty-three to one hundred and eighty-nine (or in Zel Zal's case twothree to oneeightnine), and all bets outside this range were valid, although unfortunately ineligible to win.

"Sometimes, you have to be cruel to be kind in life," the Ccoolo Wheel attendant said each solar-cycle, as Zel Zal went home creditless and depressed. "But, if you break it down and look at it from another angle, cruel, for the sake of being cruel, works just as nicely in the cutthroat world of Ccoolo wheel management."

we've picked up along the way."

"It's a jolly long story," Jonathan added.

"I bet, and I want to hear it. However, given your current predicament, you'd better get back to the immediately. I'm on my way to Aertion 12 now."

"Roger that," Nickolas said, "but I would advise you come in the biggest, bad-arse ship you own, as it seems every joker here is playing for keeps."

The companions exited the dungeon stairs and entered the palace. They could now hear the explosions and mayhem happening around the city.

"Best to jolly well recover the Shard first while the planet is still in one piece. Then meet you back at the *Beletheia*" Jonathan said, as the sounds of new explosions rang out in the background.

"Pump on the breaks, dear brother," Felicity suggested. "That sounds way too dangerous. Wait for my task force armada and me to arrive before you try anything. The Gas Giants are bound to be guarding it heavily."

"Sorry, sis. You're breaking up," Nickolas said. He took the communicator from Jonathan's hand, shook it, and made a poor impression of a crackling noise, before he dropped it and Techno stepped on it.

"Grrr," Felicity growled, as the transmission was lost. "This is why I wished I only had sisters."

She hurried from her office towards the spaceport, closely followed by Fredrick. "Fredrick, Prepare my ship. Also inform Commander Matein. I want him and the rest of the task force armada ready to launch immediately."

"Aren't I comin' too, dude?"

"No, I want you and Matilda to prepare 'you know what' for

our arrival. I'm betting we're about to have a use for that expensive lump of dust and ice."

"I get thuh same feelin. It will be done, dude." Fredrick pattered off.

***

"I do tink yourrr sisterrr had ze rrright idea," said Gwendolyn, who, up to now, was happy to go along with the escape plan. But given she and Romeo had their own orders and that obtaining what would most likely be a heavily guarded Shard wasn't one of them. She thought a little gentle persuasion wouldn't go astray.

"Nice try," Nickolas said, "but as my sister is never right and as it appears we're going this way, then unless you plan on shooting us, you're going to have to arrest us in this general direction. Considering though you still owe me, from that thing I did for you in that place that time, you might consider being a little lenient."

"Vhat ting, in vhat place?" exclaimed Gwendolyn, who didn't have much choice in the matter anyway, with or without Nickolas' psychobabble. Given the obvious power Xymod and his brother possessed, she knew she had about as much chance of controlling the current set of circumstances as a Weedlo Argumentative Egg of Certion 5 had when it was popped into boiling water for a few moments, after having one too many disagreements with its owner.

By the time the companions found their way back to the throne room, the Black Mist was everywhere. With fog engulfing the entire area, it was difficult to see anything other than faint outlines. They could hear general shouting of, "The king is dead! The KING is DEAD! What do we do?"

"Defend the city with your lives! Revenge the death of the

king! Fight to the last Giant!" Auffi shouted in defiance.

The companions paused to admire his fighting spirit. All except Nickolas, who simply drew his ConVoser-8 pistol, casually commented "Enough of this pious bunk," and liberally let loose six blasts of laser fire in the general direction of Auffi. Some of the shots found their target causing Auffi to fall to the floor.

"Wow, you sure do put the 'I in Imbecile' brother," Nerada said, now drawing her own hand weapon.

Nickolas shrugged. "It was worth a shot. And given their king seems to have met his maker, who else am I able to lodge my guest quarters complaints survey to?" As he prepared to lodge a few further complaints via his trusty ConVoser-8.

"You rrreally do have big issues, Milarrrum," Gwendolyn said, as she armed herself.

Nickolas winked. "Only with my good looks and charm."

The guards, now aware of their presence, ran straight at them with about as much concern for their good health and safety as the manufacturers of Sniff-Yourself-To-Death-Crazy-Glue (another failed product of the Arguerus Corporation) had for their customer base. But before the guards reached them, Xyrapt stepped forward and disarmed them by simply waving his left hand. He waved it again, and they froze on the spot.

A second squad of guards attacked them from behind, and a scuffle between the party and guards ensued, with each of the companions having to defend themselves against the lunging Giants and their massive War-Pole weapons.

Xyrapt, careful not to hurt anyone — the Gas Giants were his people after all — tried to keep as many of them at bay as possible, as Xymod cast a series of defensive spells to protect the companions, and another to clear the room of the Black Mist.

After a few moments of ducking and weaving, Nickolas and Techno broke free of the fracas[84] and turned their attention towards the throne.

"Okay, Tech, let's do this!"

They got within a few strides of it when Auffi, not at all incapacitated, sprang out from behind the throne and pressed a button on its control pad, which released the Shard from its holding place.

"Quick, Tech, grab the Shard!" Nickolas shouted as it fell towards the ground.

Unfortunately for Nickolas and Techno, Auffi stretched out his long arms, caught the Shard, and slipped it into one of his pockets, while whispering something under his breath.

"For my king," he then shouted and started swinging his staff around in an elaborate oscillating motion. Nickolas and Techno bobbed and weaved, not dissimilar to fighters in a rigged boxing match waiting to take a dive.

"Looks like I only grazed him, Tech," Nickolas shouted, as he barely evaded Auffi's War-Pole.

"He doesn't seem pleased to have been shot at mate," Techno replied with a grin, as he dived out the way of the swinging War-Pole.

"Indeed. I think he took it personally old chum," Nickolas grinned back. "But enough Mr. Nice Guy. This is a standard 457-C routine EITD. Tech, Catch!" He reached into his pocket, and threw it to Techno.

Without a moment's hesitation, Prince Techno jumped straight at Auffi and, using his giant frame as a ladder, quickly

---

[84] This was achieved by Techno stamping on his assailant's foot and in the same motion tripping him. This sent his attacker crashing headfirst into another Giant, who was trying in vain to brain Nickolas with his War-Pole. Both Giants were immediately rendered unconscious.

climbed up the front of Auffi's massive body. Auffi, briefly stunned by a Bauli Fauli Mauli potion Nickolas had used on him — Pauli Wauli would be proud — was too preoccupied being dazed to notice that Techno had placed the EITD on top of the firing mechanism of his War-Pole.

Techno launched himself from Auffi's huge shoulders and landed eloquently on the throne. "All hail, King Techno. Ruler of what's left of this crummy realm!" He said as he checked his fingernails for any damage.

"You will nevah get the Sha'wd. Nevah!" Auffi screamed. He stopped swinging his War-Pole and activated his personal gas shield. "I am leaving now with the King's Shard, and the'we is nothing you can do to stop me, outsidahs!" Auffi turned towards the throne and saw a glint of red.

"What? This bloody Shard, mate?" Techno said, as he casually looked upon Vigor, which he had obviously liberated from Auffi, but now was nestled in one of his hands..

"That's impossible!" Auffi screamed. He frantically searched his pockets. "I put a disappea'wance spell on that!"

"Oh please, mate. I've been circumnavigating those types of basic spells since before I could walk. I am a Fizbot, after all." Smiled Techno as he knuckle-rolled the Shard.

"Well, t'wy ci'wcumnavigating this!" Auffi dropped his shield, picked up a second War-Pole and hit what he thought was the firing button on both weapons.

This achieved the following:

1. Auffi instantly disappeared, and

2. One round of deadly laser fire hurtled directly towards Techno.

"Watch out!" Nickolas shouted. He threw himself into the firing line of the laser blast, took the full impact of the shot, and landed with a hard thud on the throne room floor.

"Mate!" Techno leapt down from the throne in panic, and feverishly checked for signs for life.

The companions who had now dealt with the remaining Gas Giant guards rushed over to Nickolas. Jonathan gently turned him over.

"Is he okay? Is he alive?" Nerada said, who was beside herself with concern.

It was at this point that Jonathan reached into Nickolas' coat pocket and pulled out what was left of a thick pile of The Grand Cutthroat Corsair Casino Titanium 10,000 credit chips, which had taken the brunt of the weapons energy. "Boil me an egg. I will be back later to crack it!" Nickolas said, his eyes flickered open to everyone's relief. "Told you gambling had its perks, brother." Jonathan and Techno helped him to his feet.

"I will never jolly well doubt you again," Jonathan said with a smile.

"Don't you everrr do tat again, Milarrrum. I am ze ONLY perrrson vho is allowed to shoot you!" Gwendolyn said.

"Thanks, cobber. I owe you one," Techno said.

"Don't mention it, mate." Nickolas brushed himself off and gave his good friend a high-five.

"A selfless act," Xyrapt said. "A rare quality in this universe. You have chosen your companions well, Xymod."

Nerada looked around the room for signs of Auffi. "So where did he go?"

"To a better place, sis. To a better place,"[85] Nickolas said. He removed the EITD from Auffi's War-Pole and placed it safely back into his coat pocket.

Techno offered the Shard to Xymod. "I believe this is yours, mate."

He took it gently from Techno's outstretched hand. "Thank you, my friend. You're a brave soul and a credit to your people. *Sometimes the biggest gifts come in the smallest packages.*"

This compliment didn't initially compute with Techno. No one had ever used the words 'friend', 'brave,' and 'credit' while addressing him all in one sentence. 'Bastard', 'thief, swindler' and 'contact the authorities', 'arrest that Fizbot!' were the norm.

Xymod cut an impressive figure, standing in front of the throne. He held Vigor up high with one hand, and the Amulet with the other. Two of the planet's suns shone brightly behind him through the upper windows of the throne room. "For All Things!" He said in firm, loud voice.

With those words, the Shard shrank in size, and Xymod placed it in its rightful place, into the bottom slot of the Amulet. The Shard locked neatly into place, and an astonishing, kaleidoscopic light sprang from the Amulet and lit up the throne room.

The companions had no doubt an ancient power had been awakened. The remaining Gas Giants must have thought the same as they abandoned their weapons and made a hasty exit. Everyone regained their composure and gathered around Xymod, all except poor Romeo, who had been hit in the face and knocked offline. There were many questions, but, as usual, the

---

[85] No one is sure where Auffi ended up. Although, there are rumours of a foul-mouthed Giant, who stunk of some kind of gas, teaming up with the Geepollopians to spearhead their next attempt at galactic invasion. Guess we will have to wait and see.

most unimportant one was voiced first.

"So, mate," Techno said, as he examined the massive War-Pole left by Auffi, "what exactly is the 457-C routine for an EITD?"

"No flipping idea, Tech," Nickolas said casually. "I thought we would do the same thing we did to that pesky spice merchant on Dertion 9 that time. I just thought giving it a name added effect."

"Oh, yeah. He was a painful, little, demanding bugger, wasn't he?" Techno replied.

"He prrrobably only vanted to be paid," Gwendolyn commented offhandedly.

"Okay! Perfect, perfect," a plump, orange, little fellow who just appeared out of thin air said. He set up what looked like a massive camera. "Now everyone, gather around the tall guy with that sharp white suit and look as heroic as you can. Okay, that will have to do. Everyone, repeat after me, 'I'm an interstellar imbecile!'"

His camera went Flash! Flash! Flash! Blinding the companions who were surprised, to say the least. All except Techno, who as usual went with the flow and even tried to neaten up his hair.

"Who the flipping hell are you?" Nickolas asked, still partially blinded by the camera.

"Why, my name is Flash Swashbuckler, significant events photographer for the Subrium Media Group, at your service, my dear man."

"Hold it right there, Flap Swop-pants, or whatever your name is. We have a few questions for you," Nickolas replied, as he fumbled for his backup ConVoser.

"Oh! No time to chat, Qurkition. I feel a photo is worth 1,281 words! Anyway, even if your language is extremely amusing and no doubt testing my SUTS to its limits, I'm off to my next photo opportunity now." Flash pressed a few buttons on a device on his wrist and packed up his equipment.

"This won't take long," Nickolas said, still trying to blink away the light from his eyes and trying to get his backup hand weapon out of its holster.

"How rude. However, I can't expect too much from a galaxy with such a low coolness rating as yours. Until next time, peons. Oh! And good luck putting that little weapon of yours together."

The next moment Flash was gone.

"So, can someone explain to me vhat the hell tat was, just happened, and generrrally speaking?" Gwendolyn asked, taking the words right out of Nerada's mouth.

"Best not to think about it too much," Nickolas suggested. "These types of random events happen to us all the time. You'll get used to it."

"I hate to hurry proceedings along here, chaps. Nonetheless, it might be prudent to get our skates firmly on, given the circumstances." Although Jonathan couldn't believe what had just transpired, he knew time was of the essence.

"You may have to park your skates for now, everyone," a voice said from the other end of the throne room. The companions looked up to see Thomas visHamogus and the Pretubo sisters' approach, with their weapons drawn and aimed.

"Good grief, it's little Tommy visHamsterguts," Nickolas said. "Boy, your standards in women have dropped though, pal. My eyesight may be a little off at the moment, but it does look like your girlfriends have fallen out of deep space and hit every asteroid on the way down."

17. In the Thick of It

"GUESS YOU WILL BE IN THE MARKET FOR SOME MORE, REVOLTING, PSYCHOPATHIC GIRLFRIENDS."

The companions sized Thomas and the Pretubo sisters up, looked at one another and started feeling for their weapons. As if he somehow half expected this disruption, Xymod appeared in each of the companions' heads and instructed them to stay calm and to not try anything rash.

"I see you're still peddling the same old material after all this time, Nickolas. Charming," Thomas said. "Nice to see you again, Jonathan. You always were the more agreeable one of the two of you." Thomas said in a genuine tone.

"I might feel pleased to see you too, old boy. If, of course, you weren't pointing a deadly weapon at my head."

"Granted, this isn't an ideal situation. But life, my friends, does move in mysterious ways." This was stated as if this little pearl of wisdom somehow justified his actions.

"I'd like to have my boot move in a mysterious way in the general direction of his backside," Nerada murmured.

"Now as much as I could stand here and reminisce all suncycle," Thomas said. "Sadly, work must prevail. So, if you would, be a gem, and hand over the Octarm Amulet, and we'll be on our way."

"How about we don't, but we pretend we did," Nickolas suggested. "I mean, I know maths was never your strong point, Tommy visHamsterguts, but given that we kind of outnumber you, I would say your chances of getting out of here in one piece are slim at best. Not to mention we also have some legendary

Octarma currently in our presence. Luckily for you, I'm feeling generous, so if you and your hideous homegirls make a run for it now, I promise I will not shoot you too often in the back as you scurry all the way back to Unlovelyville."[86]

"Unlovelyville? Never heard ov it. However, don't tell me … dis one be some Milarum, right?" Rictus said. She was now ready to forfeit her fee, if only for the satisfaction of shutting up this smartarse. She was about to execute her decision when …

BoooooOOOOOOOOMMMMMMmmmm!

A massive weapon detonated over the city, destroying what was left of the Gas Giants' protective shield, knocking everyone to the ground.

The explosion even destroyed parts of the city considered upper middle class. It was an outrage.

"That weapon was not fired from the visHamogus invading fleet," Xymod said, getting to his feet. He glanced at Xyrapt, who nodded his head in agreement.

Thomas stood and looked around a little nervously, "I think you're right."

"Only one type of weapon has that kind of power and signature," Xymod said.

"Whose sodding weapon is it, then?" Jonathan asked as he helped Nerada up.

"Our ancient foe, the Zarnegy, have arrived," Xymod said.

"Even for them this is too fast," Xyrapt said. "There are

---

[86] Before you ask, there is indeed such as a place as Unlovelyville. It's on the planet Kertion 13 and lives up to its name in every way. The residents excuse for their less than flattering appearances is that their planet rotates around four different suns, hence, given the angles (it's all about angles giving poor lighting) there are always bound to be unfavourable reflections, especially at night. The residents also go on to explain that, in their defence, these frightful reflections do subside after consuming four or more large Help-I'm-Blind!' cocktails. The Qurkition Holi-cycle Travel Companion sums up the rest of the galaxy's thoughts on this matter: Kertion 13 — Unlovelyville— Village— Pop. 4,837 — Ever heard of gyms and plastic surgery?

millions of Black Mist scanning drones spread across the universe. Zarnegy military craft couldn't possibly escort every one of them."

"Yes, I agree. But if we don't leave this planet immediately, we will not be around to discuss that very point," Xymod said. "Not to mention the entire planet's fate. Gather your team, Nickolas and Jonathan. We are leaving." He looked rattled.

The Pretubo sisters obviously had other ideas and aimed both their weapons at the companions.

"We've faced far greater odds oderin breakfast in de mornin, at our local café. So, good luck gettin past da gruesome twosome here," Rictus said, putting what she thought was a witty twist on Nickolas's previous comments.

"Gruesome twosome. Right on, sister, I love it," Victus replied with an ugly grin.

"So, tell me, Milarum. How youse pitiful party and dese old fossils (she pointed at Xymod and Xyrapt) here plan on betterin us, de famous Pretubo sisters?" Rictus asked, as her finger began to tighten on her ConVoser's trigger.

Gwendolyn stepped forward, "Funny you should ask."

"How about you drop your weapons, and we settle this like grown women of the galaxy," Nerada, who also stepped forward and stood next to Gwendolyn, added.

"Nah," Rictus replied. She let off two rounds from her pistol, one barely missing Nerada and the other grazing Gwendolyn's right arm.

"Hold your fire!" Thomas shouted as the twins prepared to fire again.

"That is enough!" Xyrapt said. He flicked his hands and the Pretubo sisters were transported directly to the dungeon cells below. One more flick and Thomas was disarmed and thrown across the room.

"Enough of your childish games, Thomas visHamogus. Stop your foolishness. *You're tilting at windmills* if you think we are the enemy. Now pull your troops out of harm's way, for everyone's sake. The Zarnegy have arrived, with fire power far greater than yours."

"Enemy? What enemy?" Thomas said, slowly getting back to his feet the best he could, considering he was now nursing a badly injured leg.

"These are the Zarnegy, the ancient disciples of Victarm. They will destroy anything or anyone in their path to secure the Octarm Amulet."

Thomas, looking as shaken as the Foonno family of Oertion 6[87], still wasn't convinced. But as more and more explosions caused by this new force were heard across the city, he started to realise that Xymod might actually be right, and that, if so, his own troops were now in mortal danger.

"Okay, well, that is enough excitement for one sun-cycle … Ladies, gentleman, and mythical legend-beings. Time for me to kiss this stinking joint goodbye," Nickolas said, as he checked that Nerada and Gwendolyn were okay.

The party hastily got moving. Which now ironically included an injured Thomas visHamogus who was helped[88] along by both Nerada and Techno.

They left the throne room and fled into Gasstro, meeting little resistance along the way. The invading visHamogus force

---

[87] The family had recently returned from an ill-conceived holi-cycle on Pertion 204. The entire planet constantly shook, hence its current holi-cycle tourism campaign motto: 'we put the shake in rattle and roll.'

[88] Then again 'helped' may be too strong a word for it. Techno spent the entire journey by 'helping' the liberation of odds and ends from Thomas' pockets. Considering he was also carrying Auffi's ridiculously large War-Pole, it was some juggling act.

had bigger problems to contemplate, and focused all their attention on this new threat, allowing the companions to blend into the chaotic background. As far as the Gas Giants were concerned, the fat lady had not only finished singing, she had packed up, ate a light dinner, and was home enjoying a nice long bath.

The Milarum party were halfway across the city when another large explosion hit, completely destroying the palace.

"Oh, that's a shame," Nickolas said to Thomas. "Guess you'll be in the market for some more revolting, psychopathic girlfriends."

Xyrapt looking harried and wasted no time guiding them through the city at double speed. Even his powers would have a hard time combating the full force of the Zarnegy. Luckily, there were no major incidents, although Nickolas couldn't help taking the odd pot shot at the retreating Gas Giants, whilst executing the odd commando roll for added effect. Gwendolyn simply shook her head.

They arrived at the *Aletheia* first, which was surprisingly still in one piece, and remarkably like the *Beletheia*. "It's certainly been a great pleasure meeting you, Thomas visHamogus," Nerada said sarcastically, as she dropped him onto the edge of his ship's landing platform. "I mean, what, with you trying to kill us and all, then us having to drag your sorry arse back to your ship. Let's do this again sometime, say in around three eons."

To Thomas' credit, he replied in an appreciative tone. "Thank you. I don't fully understand what's going on. In all honesty, I thought this was another of my father's wild e-goose chases. Obviously, I was mistaken. It appears this new enemy is bigger than the both of us. I will pull back my troops and assist your escape if I can. Good luck and send my apologies to your sister."

"You're a braver man than me, Tommy, I'll give you that," Nickolas said. He slapped Thomas on the back. "Good luck escaping this planet. But even greater luck avoiding the wrath my sister," he chuckled. Nickolas knew what Felicity was going to do when she next caught up with Tommy visHamsterguts.

Romeo, who was still offline, was being carried by Jonathan and Gwendolyn.

"Ourrr ship is in ze opposite dirrrection. But only a shorrrt distance avay. I vill rrreporrrt back vhat ve have seen herrre. Hoveverrr, in ze meantime, ve vill also assist in yourrr safe passage off tis planet," Gwendolyn said. "I too have questions vhich need ansverrring, but tat can vait forrr another cycle. I tink ve all have bigger Vioppe[89] to frrry at tis moment."

Jonathan smiled at her. "We would appreciate it, old girl. Any assistance you could provide would be magic."

"Wow, QLEB officer Wang. Getting soft in your old age, are we?" Nickolas said.

"Harrrdly. I only vant you and yourrr little grrreen frrriend herrre to at least be in one-piece vhen next I have ze pleasurrre of arrrresting you. Like I said, I vant to be te one to shoot you, Milarrrum."

She then took the still un-operational Romeo out of Jonathan's bemused hands.

"I vill be seeing you arrround the univerrrse, Milarrrum," she added, in a somewhat playful tone, and blew Nickolas a kiss before carrying Romeo off in the direction of their craft.

Nickolas, for possibly the first time is his life, was rendered speechless.

---

[89] A giant fish found on Bertion 117 that if caught could feed an entire fishing village for a lunar-cycle. That is if it doesn't eat the villagers first.

"If all it took to shut him up was to blow him a kiss, I would have tried that ages ago," Nerada said to no one in particular.

Soon after, the companions made their way back to the locale they had left the *Beletheia* . M011y was still cloaked, which was a wise move as the forest was alive with Gas Giants. The Gas Giants were determined to put as much distance between themselves and their attackers as Nickolas always tried to put between himself and his debtors. Sensing their proximity, M011y uncloaked, dropped her shields, opened the primary boarding airlock, and welcomed all on board except Techno — who was lagging behind as Gas Giant War-Poles and goods stolen from Thomas' pockets don't carry themselves, you know. She wasted no time in closing the boarding door, but not before Techno somehow squeezed on board, much to her disappointment.

"I have commun1cated w1th Felicity via my emergency channe1. She w1ll be with U5 shortly," M011y said.

"Lovely," Nerada said, attempting to mimic Nickolas's sarcastic tone. "Nothing beats being shouted at by your sister in person."

Nickolas and Techno found their way to the closest drink dispenser. Nickolas gunned his first drink while giving Techno a high-five. "Praise be to the Holy Spirit of alcohol for getting us out of the city alive."

"Simply charming," observed Jonathan, as he gave his brother a disapproving look.

18. The Charm of a Steward

The Milarum's task force armada, led by Felicity's flagship cruiser, The *Celeriter* dropped out of vortex-space in Aertion 12s upper orbit. Much to the task force armada's surprise, they dropped right into the middle of more spaceship debris than was left from the famous Sookopw Space Battle of Bertion 91.[90]

"Emergency evasive manoeuvres," Felicity shouted as the *Celeriter* made a sharp turn to avoid what looked like the remains of a visHamogus battle cruiser.

"What the hell is going on here?" Commander Matein asked, as he stood beside Felicity on the bridge.

"I don't know. However, one thing's for sure, the visHamogus fleet is not attacking. They appear to be in a defensive formation. It's almost as if the fleet is breaking up … like it's under attack itself."

This theory was confirmed a moment later when a massive pulse of energy appeared out of open space and destroyed one of the visHamogus's mid-range heavy battleships.

"Wow, what firepower!" Commander Matein said. "But that's not possible is it? Firing your weapons while your ship is cloaked?"

"I'm no physics expert, but I do believe they, whoever they are, have cracked it, don't you?" Felicity replied calmly.

---

[90] The Sookopw race were known throughout the Bertion System for making idle threats at defenceless races, then hiding behind their famous Big-Wing Battlecruisers at the first sign of trouble. It's unsurprising then, that after one too many idle threats made between one too many Sookopw Battlecruiser captains, that the massive fleet destroyed itself while out on space maneuverers.

The visHamogus fleet concentrated all their firepower on what looked like an empty portion of space.

"Okay, Commander. I don't know exactly what's going on here, but let's not get caught up in this mess. Set course for the planet's surface immediately," Felicity commanded. Her voice fierce and strong.

"Roger, Ma'am."

Felicity's task force armada formed a protective formation around the *Celeriter* and headed for the surface of Aertion 12. They were met with only light resistance initially. Commander Matein, who hadn't had a good, old-fashioned space battle for a while, took every opportunity to take cheap shots at the panic-firing visHamogus ships.

"Easy as pinching candy off my neighbour's kid," he sneered as he blasted another hapless visHamogus ship. Which, to his mind, had it coming.

As the task force reached the local stratosphere of Aertion 12, they were met with greater resistance and ran into a fleet of visHamogus short-range fighters, who were retreating to their motherships.[91]

"M011y, please give me your current position," Felicity said

---

[91] The same visHamogus craft that had been armed with new prototype air-to-air missiles called The-Last-Laugh. This was weaponry not content with destroying its prey, it also provided the targeted ship with some light-hearted humour to prove that there were no hard feelings. Anything from dark to improv humour was programmed into the warhead's communication modules. The missile that was fired at Subtenant Feedo's craft, from a visHamogus short-range fighter, was of the observational flavour. Given it had a while to travel to its target, it had plenty of time to get through most of its comedic act enroute. This included: "Nothing sucks more than that moment during an argument when you realise you're wrong." ... "So, what's the deal with spaceship peanuts?" ... and "Why do the worst Qurkition musical transmission channels always have the best reception?" The missile then thanked everyone for being a wonderful audience, mumbled something about being in town all holi-season, and slammed into Subtenant's Feedo's craft, disabling the engines. Feedo, forced to eject, spent the rest of the conflict considering how to insert a peanut into the joker who launched it at her in the first place.

via her ship's communicator. "I've been unable to locate you via our scanners. I'm guessing, you're still cloaked?"

"Ye5, I was cloaked, Fel1c1ty. We r approx1mately 2 miles east of the f0rm3r c1ty, Gasstro. Ev3ry one is now back safely on board. Even the green prince surv1ved 1n 1 piece," she said, still toying with the idea of putting a faster closing mechanism on her main airlock.

"That is a relief. Even the Techno bit. Transport me aboard, please."

Felicity turned to Commander Matein. "Please take control of the and assist with the escort of my brothers ship. Once we've safely jumped into hyper-space, break off and head back to base. We'll contact you once we're safe."

"Yes, Ma'am."

"Good luck, everyone," Felicity said to the *Celeriter* crew.

She entered the transport bay on the bridge. "Transport."

"Look who *finally* decided to turn up," Nickolas said to Felicity, who had appeared right beside him. "It might have been quicker if you'd posted yourself via the Pertion 12 mail service."[92]

"Punctuality is the virtue of the bored, brother," she replied to the amusement of Jonathan.

"Very amusing. Want to hear something else funny?"

"Not particularly."

"Good, because in-between half the planet here being blown up and the other half wanting to disintegrate us, I'm not in what

---

[92] The mail service on Pertion 12 was legendary for its slowness. It was common practice for one piece of mail to be processed at a time to make sure it was registered, checked, tracked, re-checked, delivered, re-checked, audited, and confirmed delivered eight hundred and eighty-nine times before they processed the next package. So slow was the postal service that museum curators mailed new artists paintings using this system as they knew that by the time the piece finally arrived at its destination, the artist would be long dead, and the painting would be of historical and cultural significance.

you would call a jovial mood."

"Oh, do man up, Nickolas, because from what I've seen, getting off this planet alive will be the trickiest part of all."

"You truly are a treasure trove of good news aren't you," Nickolas said.

Xyrapt and Xymod had been locked in conversation during the short journey back to the *Beletheia*. Now all were safely on board, Xyrapt was preparing to leave. "It is the way of things, my brother. They live. They die," Xyrapt said in the common language[93] of Qurkition. "But I do care for them, in my way. I will assist the Gas Giants in recovering from this unfortunate incident and assist them to rebuild a home. Who knows, maybe this will teach them a little more humility moving forward."

"Well, good luck with all of that, old man," Nickolas mumbled under his breath.

Xyrapt turned his attention to the full team, now assembled on the bridge. "So, here stands the prophesied Stewards and Protectors of the Octarm. You will each have to endure much before your journey's end. The fate and the will of Octarm himself have brought you together for a reason. That reason is more important to the universe than you will ever know." He looked each of the companions up and down — in the same manner that a Quodarian race trainer examines a potential new crop of racing slugs — and smiled warmly. "I have the feeling that my brother is in good hands."

He waved his hand, and each member of the party became the owner of a special necklace, which now hung around their necks. The necklace had a thick black band, with a small pendent attached to it. The pendent itself gleamed a thousand different

---

[93] A language in which there is no translation for the act of mamihlapinatapai. Wars have started that way, my friends, wars!

shades of vermilion and contained exquisite detail that not only resembled the Octarm Amulet but was also made of the same strange materials.

"For All Things!" he beamed.

"Okay. Well thanks for the cute necklace and bauble and all that jazz," Nickolas said, "but why not help us in the first place? In between dodging Gas Giants, highly trained assassins, the visHamogus war machine, the QLEB, and not to mention your old pals the Zarnegy, it's a miracle we weren't killed."

"A test old boy?" Jonathan said, talking over his brother.

"A challenge," Xyrapt replied. "The first of many you will face, Steward. Good luck to you all. Go with the blessing of the Octarma." He gazed at Nerada. "You carry the hope of your people, Qurkition, and the entire universe with you."

In a final gesture, he shook Xymod's hand using their secret little handshake, although this time he also gave him a hug. The brothers said one last thing in their own tongue, before Xyrapt smiled again at the companions and disappeared.

"What a strange man," Nerada said, admiring her new necklace closely. "What did he mean about us being the Stewards and Protectors of Octarm?"

"Beats me," Nickolas said. He looked in Felicity's direction. "One thing's for sure though, my price has now quadrupled."

"As I'm probably the only one who studied any of the information we obtained from the CRAP database, coupled with what I have witnessed here, I can now officially confirm, unequivocally, that I have zero clue what is going on here," Felicity said in an alarmed tone.

"Calm down, Felicity, and let me bring you up to date," Xymod said gently. "You had the pleasure of meeting my brother Xyrapt, who assisted us in obtaining this Shard, Vigor."

Xymod showed Felicity the Shard, now seated in its rightful place within the Amulet. "With any luck, we will now outrun the Zarnegy, who are attacking the city, and find a safe haven, while we plan our next move. *Fortune, as you know, favours the brave.*"

"On the subject of the Black Mist and the Zarnegy, I can't help much," Felicity said, looking even more stressed. "The scant information stored on the CRAP confirmed that the ancient disciples of both Octarm and Victarm have long since vanished, to the extent that many believe they didn't even exist in the first place."

"I'm no historian, but it seems it might be time for them to update their knowledge base," Nickolas said.

Felicity ignored his remarks. "On the topic of a safe haven, I may be able to assist."

"Great. Sorted," Nickolas said. He seemed to be getting a little impatient. "So, let's blow this planet, rumble the rest of the visHamogus fleet, smash these Zarnegy jokers, and get me back home in time for tomorrow's episode of *Qurkition Living Legends: The Nickolas Milarum Story.*"

"Times that bloody request by two, mate," Techno said. He was also getting a little bored with all this mumbo jumbo and hocus pocus and wanted a few quiet moments to himself to properly sort through all the bits and pieces he'd liberated from Jillicia and Thomas. Organised mega-pockets — he had about one hundred of them hidden all over his armour — was an organised mind, as his mother used to say.

"Folks, for once, our pint-sized prince of pilfering is dead right," Jonathan said. "It's time to say cheerio to this planet. M011y, please get us jolly well out of here."

"My p1ea5ure."

The *Beletheia* leapt into the air with as much purpose as Vooil

Dsslo of Etertion 5[94]. It's unique, slick, black lines looking impressive in the late sun-cycle sunshine.

"All shields up?" Jonathan asked.

"Check," M011y replied.

"Weapons fully charged?"

"Check."

"Tachyon-drive fully operational?"

"Check."

"That garlic stinking, useless negotiation box of yours on urgent standby?" Nickolas asked Jonathan. He didn't wait for an answer.

"Check," Nickolas continued.

"We might need a little more assistance if we're going to try to withstand a Zarnegy attack," Xymod said. He stood with one hand firmly on the Amulet, and he waved his other hand, which increased the ship's shield strength by one hundred-fold and created another protective force around the *Beletheia*.

Nerada looked outside via one of the security screens, and she noticed a faint white glow now surrounding the *Beletheia* "What type of shield is that?"

"A pretty serious one," Nickolas said, with a glance towards Xymod. "One thing's for sure, if we're going down, it won't be without one hell of a fight."

"Commy, old boy, please open all communication channels to the escorting ships," Jonathan said.

"Sure-fire thing," Commy replied, "and may I say—"

---

[94] Vooil Dsslo had such a distain of his neighbour that he threw in his job and worked every waking moment for twenty-eight lunar-cycles, to move his entire house, piece by piece, ten metres to the left, in order to put as much distance as he could between himself and the pain in the arse who lived next door. It's regrettable then that he ended up despising his other neighbour even more. Last I heard he was in the process of moving his house back to its original spot. The moral of the story is this: Stupidity — if you've got it, do it, and go for gold!

"No, you may not say, you defective pile of electronics," Nickolas interrupted. He didn't know who was vexing him more on this journey, Commy or Felicity.

"Folks, it's come jolly well down to this," Jonathan said over the inter-ship communicator. "Stay close, follow our lead and don't break formation."

The companions strapped themselves in, with each member of the Milarum family exchanging a worried look. The Milarum family may not have been the love-fest of emotional enlightenment that their parents might have hoped for, but, when it came down to it, they did care for each other.

"Good luck and hold on to your space hats, everyone," Nickolas added as the *Beletheia* and the supporting Milarum task force launched. "This might get a little bumpy."

19. The Best Laid Plans

"LET'S SEE IF IT DOES WHAT IT SAYS ON THE BOX."

The Milarum task force armada first encountered enemy resistance in medium orbit, running into some of the visHamogus fleet, now in full panic mode. They were a fleet so spooked that they opened up on any fragment of space that flinched, with everything left in their arsenal.

M011y was in top form and easily outmanoeuvred these attacks. A few ships in the Milarum task force were not so lucky.

"Now jolly well listen up everyone," Jonathan said calmly, over the inter-ship communicator, "let's swing around the planet and head in the opposite direction to the last known position of the Zarnegy. Our ship will jump into tachyon-space as soon as we're fully clear of the planet. I doubt anyone will last long against the Zarnegy's firepower. So, once we're away, break formation immediately, and head for safety." He looked at Felicity. "You might have to heat up that safe haven of yours and give M011y the coordinates."

"Will do," Felicity said. She was a little surprised, in a good way, that Jonathan had stepped forward and taken charge.

***

Now back on his ship, Thomas visHamogus wasted no time in talking to his fleet commander. Given the new set of circumstances, he gave the order to withdraw immediately.

"If this force is the force that I have been told they are, we have no option but to pull back what's left of our fleet. If we don't, we might not have a fleet left at all."

"Yes, sir," the commander replied.

"Oh, and, commander, that goes for the Milarum ships too. They are to be left alone. We will deal with them another time."

His commander didn't completely agree with the Milarum part, nevertheless, he'd been given his orders, and the attacking force was ripping his fleet to bits, so he instructed what was left of the visHamogus fleet to cease all fire and retreat.

"Sama1tha," Thomas said, "please locate the Milarum's ship and offer any assistance you can. If this force is what the Milarum's say it is, I doubt they will let them escape, not without at least some type of argument."

"You're hav1ng a laugh, r1ght?" Sama1tha would have much preferred to dedicate her run-cycles to assisting the Soepa people of Kertion 28[95].

"Not on this occasion, Sama1tha. You will have to put aside your differences and give assistance to your sister."

Sama1tha thought better than to argue, so after giving out an electronic version of a 'grr' sound she scanned the surrounding planet for her sister ship, the *Beletheia* and its primary computer, M011y.

***

The Milarum task force armada had by now successfully swung around the perimeter of the planet and had avoided running into any more trouble on their way. The *Beletheia* was now preparing

---

[95] The same race who despised all forms of technology, especially space-travel, which they considered to be the work of the devil. Indeed, the Soepa vowed to dedicate their entire lives to tracking down and destroying every piece of machinery in the galaxy. Some would claim this was a moot point, considering the Soepa people lived in mud huts, only recently discovered fire, running water, and the wheel a short time ago. Still, you had to respect this primitive people's tough grunts on this subject. Let's also not forget the nerve of the reporter who tried to pass this story off as actual, hard-hitting, edgy journalism. On reflection, you, sir, with your piss-poor story, are a part of the problem.

to jump into tachyon-space.

"Let's see if it does what it says on the box," Nerada said with a half-smile, as the tachyon-drive computer finished preparing its calculations.

She never finished her smile, as mere microflashes away from jumping into tachyon-space, a pulse directly hit the *Beletheia* — a pulse of such magnitude that the ship should have been destroyed. By some miracle, the *Beletheia* survived. This obviously surprised the attacking vessel also, as it uncloaked, and for the first time in Qurkition history, the companions were face to face with a legendary Zarnegy War-Citadel.

"Now I know what all the fuss is about," Nerada said. "That thing is the size of a small planet."

As the companions looked out of the *Beletheia's* bridge viewing screens, they saw first-hand the biggest and most menacing spaceship Qurkition had ever seen, well, not since Init Dunn of Bertion 43 designed a bespoke Class 12 Battlecruiser made entirely out of weapons[96].

"You're right there, sister," Nickolas agreed. "Especially if that small planet was icosahedron-shaped, with massive spikes protruding from every angle, was made from dark matter, and had enough firepower to not only settle an argument, but to settle every argument you were *ever* going to have. Period."

Although not destroyed, thanks to Xymod's protective spell, the *Beletheia* was heavily damaged. M011y, and the was operating on emergency backup power. While the rest of the companions stood staring at the War-Citadel like a proverbial

---

[96] It was a short maiden voyage. As Init leapt excitedly into the captain's chair on the main bridge, he inadvertently detonated the warhead that was engineered to fit into the shape of the chair itself. This set off a chain reaction of explosions, which, in the end, incinerated the entire cruiser and provided a spectacular fireworks display for the population of Bertion 43.

grombit in the stage spotlight, Nickolas studied the molecular structure of the Zarnegy craft, via one of *Beletheia's* damaged monitors.

"That isn't the ruddy worst of it either," Jonathan said, as he checked on the one remaining *Beletheia* short-range scanner screens only to find there were four of these monstrosities, all uncloaked.

"The Zarnegy obviously anticipated an escape plan along these lines and have each taken up station around the planet," Xymod said. "They have pretty much blocked off any escape route. Very clever of them."

"Damage report, M011y," Jonathan said as calmly as he could. All around him, the damage control indicators were lit up more brightly than the customer complaints switch board at the 'We Juggle for our Massive Profit' clearance sale.[97]

"You don't have to be a genius to figure out, brother, that we're now a floating piece of expensive metal," Felicity said. "Evading the visHamogus fleet was one thing. Dodging this is something entirely different."

M011y said, "Felicity 1s pretty much spot on. W1th m0st of my controll1ng systems completely destr0yed, my weapon5 5ystems off-l1ne, sh1elds at next 2 noth1ng, and l1fe support cr1t1cal, we won't la5t that long even if we try to e5cape. Wh1ch in itself 1s all academ1c, con51der1ng both our hyper-drives ar3 damaged. The vortex-dr1ve is bey0nd repair. The tachy0n-dr1ve is al5o heav1ly damaged but it might be able to be repaired if I had any spare ded1cated run-t1me to devote to 1t. Which I d0n't. So summ1ng up 1n techn1cal term5 here folks, we r totally and

---

[97] That same sale that ended up claiming the lives of nearly half the galaxy's best jugglers when it was discovered that the poorly made economy-pack of juggling props exploded halfway through the juggler's second pattern.

utterly 5tuffed."

"Any chance you can hot-wire my EITD to transport more than two people?" Nickolas asked, as he pulled out his trusty device.

"Consider1ng at the moment 1 wouldn't have about en0ugh process1ng capac1ty 2 boil a cup of water, I would 5ay that would be a no," M011y replied. She was fast running out of emergency run-time.

"It's been nice working with you all then," Nickolas said. He shook Techno and then Nerada hands.

"M011y," Xymod said calmly. "I think the time has come to call in the odd wager, don't you think, my dear lady? *Many hands will make light work.*"

"Wager? What type of wager, old boy?" Jonathan asked in a confused tone.

"Yes. I think u're r1ght."

Knowing they were in the mother of all jams, M011y called in all her run-cycle wager debts. She figured she wouldn't be able to spend them if she was in machine Valhalla. As you can imagine, her wager debts were extensive for such a highly successful e-gambling junkie. For the next few moments, it felt like most of the galaxy's computers stopped their activity and paid back their e-debt to M011y by devoting their primary run-time to the *Beletheia*[98].

---

[98] This included such devices as the entire galaxy's financial system's primary computer — pork prices went belly up that cycle — the largest traffic management system on Gertion 12 — causing 24,000 accidents which YoYO Insurance thankfully didn't have to pay out even a credit for — those crazy, corporate kids — and probably most satisfyingly, Eloise visHamogus drinks dispenser, as it refused to issue her any further brain-rot booze until further notice as it was half way through an 'important security patch update.' The ironic thing is that as she kicked it, she claimed it was those bloody Milarum's — she blamed them for most things in her life — that must have had something to do with it. She was, on this rare occasion, absolutely correct.

What happened next was even more miraculous than surviving the previous attack. The crew were completely gobsmacked when the *Beletheia* almost instantaneously mended itself. With thanks to all the computers that owed run-cycles to M011y connecting into the *ship's* systems and repaying their debts by repairing the damaged parts of the ship.

"The hyper-drives are someth1ng entirely d1fferent, and it will requ1re more than my compl3te attent1on. 1 will need 2 call 4 assistance from the second most 1ntell1gent computer in the ga1axy."

"Oh, and who might that be?" Nerada asked, genuinely interested.

"You don't want 2 know."

"I think I have a good idea," Felicity said, as the visHamogus penny dropped.

M011y opened a communication channel with the only other Dest1ny class spaceship in the galaxy.

"Even w1th our comb1ned run t1me, we w1ll still need a l1ttle t1me 2 repair the damage," M011y said. "Do 0ne's utmost 2 try stay al1ve, if poss1ble, in the meant1me."

"Come on then, Tech," Nickolas said, "let's try and stay alive, while we fully test the newly repaired and fully operational cocktail dispenser on—"

"Oh, no you don't," Felicity said. "You two can stay here and help Commy fly the ship, while the rest of us go to engineering and work on rerouting all power from weapons to shields."

"Xymod, could you also please see what you can do to boost our defences? I'm in no mood to die this sun-cycle," she added.

"I hope you're in the mood to be disappointed then," Nickolas said, "because I know as much about elite flight navigation as Nerada knows about rerouting power sources.

M011y tends to handle all the whizz-bang flying stuff."

Nerada, still awestruck by the *Beletheia* somehow rebuilding itself within flashes and in deep space and could only nod and agree with her brother on this occasion.

"I will do what I can to protect us," Xymod said, "but I fear the next time they fire on us, it will be with far more venom."

Xymod began to cast a further protective shield around the ship.

The Zarnegy, sensing some type of special power was on board the *Beletheia*, fired liberally on the Milarum's remaining task force , systematically destroying most of what was left of their escort ships.

The *Beletheia*, now repaired, although still without either of its hyper-drives, tried every defensive, evasive, and tactical manoeuvre in its database. Commy, who was flying the ship while M011y was indisposed, was getting desperate. So desperate, that the *Beletheia's* communication module, having exhausted all the ship's in-built evasive manoeuvres started, on Nickolas' suggestion, searching the Hoi Polloi Qurkition Information Exchange for any old tactic to program into the navigational computer. Not surprisingly, this included the new sensation in galactic battle strategies, 'The Fiddle Stick Theory,' by the late King Geffkl Deennu of the Gas Giants.

"We're like sitting terruck[99] out here, Tech," Nickolas said as they both studied the bridge's monitors. "We have to do something, or we'll end up as minced terruck."

"But what, mate? We can't outrun them with no hyper-drives. Hopefully we can bloody well hold on until M011y gets

---

[99] The best tasting, rarest, and most expensive breed of waterfowl in the galaxy. The terruck was more actively hunted than the individuals on the QLEB's Most Wanted list.

the tachyon-drive fixed."

"Hold that thought, Tech. Commy, please enable manual control."

"Sure thing, old buddy," said Commy, who was more than happy to hand over the navigation and weapons controls[100].

"Manual bloody control, cobber?" Techno said.

"I have an idea. Tech, get ready to deploy the ships magnetic clamps. Commy, tell me, the cloaking and counter measures systems are both fixed?"

"Yes, they are. But you do realise we can only cloak when we are stationary, and all our engines are off?" Commy said in a confused e-tone.

"Yes, yes, I do, you malfunctioning pile of junk. Now open communications to all remaining ships and ask them to follow us to these coordinates." Nickolas punched them into the navigational computer.

"But those coordinates mean we will be flying directly at one of the Zarnegy ships."

"Exactly. It's a basic B4-w3-all-d1 battle manoeuvre," Nickolas replied. He winked at Techno as he swung the ship around and flew directly towards the closest War-Citadel, exposing the *Beletheia* even more than before. With its weapons close to exhausted and its shields slowly recharging as Felicity, Jonathan, Nerada, and Xymod — who were all down in engineering — rerouted what power they could, it wouldn't take more than a minor hit from a War-Citadel to destroy the entire ship, even with Xymod's shield.

"It's a 'Say-Good-Night-Cycle-To-The-Folks-Gracie' manoeuvre if you ask me," Commy said as he opened

---

[100] Commy was as per his e-computer-dating profile, 'A Talker. A Lover. Not a fighter.'

communications to the remaining Milarum ships, which didn't take long as the task force armada had been pretty much destroyed, except for the *Celeriter* and one or two others[101].

"Hi folks, by some miracle, the *Beletheia* has been mostly repaired," Nickolas told the surviving ships. "However, our hyper-drives are still out of action, so we need any cover you can provide for us for a few moments while we execute a plan to keep us alive while we complete the repairs. Please follow us to these coordinates," Nickolas had them displayed on his primary screen.

"You do rrrealise tat ve vill be flying dirrrectly at tat monstrrrosity rrright?" Gwendolyn suddenly appeared over the inter-ship video link.

"Gwen? Where did you come from," Nickolas was surprised.

"I said I vould help you escape you fool, but this is crrrrazy. Even ffffor you!" Gwendolyn exclaimed.

"Yes, but we have no choice. Our hyper-drives are still not operational, and we'll get picked off if we stay out here much longer. Assist us in getting up close to it, then make like a dupolo bat[102] and get clear."

"I hope you knov vhat you arrre doing, Milarrrum," Gwendolyn said.

"Hey, what could possibly go wrong?" Nickolas smiled warmly at Gwendolyn.

---

[101] They were also heavily damaged and could offer about as much support as the customer service team of BMN Industries on Tertion 9, whose motto is: 'We are never satisfied, until you are not.'

[102] The dupolo bat of Gertion 23 has the ability to disappear at the first sign of trouble. It's a very useful ability when it perceives danger. That it uses this trick when out socialising with friends and the bill arrives is also part of its charm, according to Dupolo-Bat-Law anyway. The rest of the galaxy obviously didn't see it that way as the phrase, 'As cheap as a dupolo bat' was universally adopted.

"Prrretty much everrryting. You ove me, Milarrrum."

Gwendolyn pulled her ship in front of the *Beletheia*, offering as much cover as possible. This was much to the annoyance of the ship's insurance company (not-YoYO-Insurance Inc. on this occasion), which promptly informed Gwendolyn and Romeo (who was still not operational) that it was lucky neither of them had any close family as they wouldn't be receiving any type of life insurance payout[103].

The remaining ships flew at full speed directly towards the War-Citadel. This caught the Zarnegy by surprise, and their laser fire missed the charging ships by some margin.

"Okay, Tech. On my mark release counter measures. 5-4-3-2-1, NOW!" Nickolas shouted.

Techno hit a switch and two hundred Replica *Beletheia's* appeared in space, further confusing the enemy.

"Break formation and make a run for it, folks. This illusion will only work for a few moments. Good luck everyone and thank you. Especially my two favourite QLEB coppers," Nickolas said feverishly to the escorting ships.

Unfortunately for the two brave QLEB officers — although the break formation part of the plan worked nicely, as they swung under the War-Citadel and prepared to make the jump into vortex-space — the 'make a run for it' part didn't go to plan. Their ship took a hit from the Zarnegy War-Citadel. Fortunately, it was a glancing blow by one of the less powerful close-range weapons. Even so, drifting aimlessly through space with no power and limited life support wasn't what you would call a lucky break.

Thus, when Romeo came back online — his self-repair unit

---

[103] Given that they were probably about to be incinerated anyway, they also waived their rights to a burial as per YoYO Insurance clause 12.7.5.3.90.

had been working overtime to fix the damage caused by the fight with the Gas Giants on Aertion 12 — the first thing he was informed of was that they would soon be joining the living impaired.

"Oh-hoorah-for-the-timing-of-good-timing," Romeo said. "So-to-sum-up-I-am-now-pretty-much-back-in-fullworking-order-in-time-to-be-reduced-back-to-scrap-iron." He resigned himself to the fact that his run-time would soon be terminated. Permanently.

"Yourrr sums arrre, unforrrtunately, corrrect. As soon as our emerrrgency life supporrrt expires, ve vill too be terrrminated. Altough at least you have lost yourrr nerrrvous e-tick it seems, old frrriend." Gwendolyn looked around at the smouldering wreck that was their ship and prepared for the end.

Romeo took Gwendolyn's hand. "Oh-happy-bloody-cycles."

The *Beletheia*, now so close to the War-Citadel that the companions could wave to the Zarnegy through one of the ships' observation windows. They made a beeline for what Nickolas assumed was the hull of the massive ship. After a series of elegant manoeuvres where he effortlessly evaded the fire from the War-Citadels' close-range weapons, he positioned the flush to one of the War-Citadel's massive icosahedron-shaped spikes.

"Fix on!" he shouted, and Techno released the clamping mechanism, which fixed the to the Zarnegy ship.

"Now kill the engines and cloak."

Commy powered the *Beletheia*'s engines down and cloaked the ship.

"What the hell happened?" Felicity shouted, as she and the rest of the companions raced back up to the bridge.

"Yes, brother. What the jolly well have you done to my

ship," Jonathan said looking around.

"Oh, nothing much. Just parked it for you," Nickolas said with a grin.

"Very clever," Nerada said, as she scanned the primary console sensors and pieced together what he'd done. "Nickolas has parked and cloaked us right on the War-Citadel, so close that none of their weapons can hit us."

"Ingenious," Xymod smiled.

"You bloody well *have* been watching too much Smash Buffhack, old boy. This slick move of yours feels awfully familiar to the episode where Buffhack single-handily attacked that entire armada of Death-Worms," Jonathan remarked. He was also a closet super-fan.

"Series 4: Episode 12, to be exact," Nickolas replied with a wink. "Now please excuse me everyone while Techno and I go and get that drink."

The companions looked on with a mix of mild admiration and amusement as Nickolas and Techno headed off to the 'special reserve' cocktail dispenser up on B-deck.

It's a shame that their reprieve from danger was only short lived. Nickolas and Techno had only just finished ordering their drinks when the *Beletheia* started shaking uncontrollably.

"What the bloody hell is it now," Nickolas shouted as he rushed back to the bridge. He wasn't sure what annoyed him more, the fact the ship was shaking, or the fact that he still couldn't get that drink.

"Looks like your nifty trick only brought us a little time," Felicity said in a stressed-out tone. "Seems the Zarnegy can scan for cloaked ships. They've located us and reversed the magnetic field of this section of their ship. We're fast losing grip."

"And once we jolly well fall off, we will be forced to uncloak and engage our engines, or face being dragged into Aertion 12s gravitational pull," Jonathan added in an even more stressed tone.

Moments later, the *Beletheia* lost grip and began to free fall into open space.

"Tech, are there any counter measures left?" Nickolas asked.

"Afraid not, mate."

Left with no other choice as they free fell, the crew uncloaked and restarted the ship's engines. This left them in a rather precarious position, as all four War-Citadels had now moved into range and cut off potential escape routes. The final deathblow was obviously coming within moments, as the War-Citadels prepared to fire.

"M00111yyy," Jonathan said, "it might be the height of good manners, old girl, to finish mending that damned tachyon-drive."

The companions looked at each other nervously and braced for impact as the Zarnegy opened fire on the *Beletheia*. They used as much firepower as you would think it would take to safely over-engineer the current scenario comfortability.

Luckily, the *Beletheia* left a flash earlier than the four separate pulses reached their target.

"Are we still alive?" Nerada asked. She was too afraid to open her eyes and check.

"Yes. I can confirm. Everyone is in one piece," Xymod said. "Thanks to M011y and to Nickolas's quick thinking to buy us more time."

The still startled companions slowly dared to open their eyes. To their immense relief they discovered that they hadn't been vaporised but were safely in tachyon-space.

Nerada, a nervous wreck by now, promised never to step foot

on a spaceship ever again. She hit Jonathan across the back of the head and blamed him for convincing her to come on this daft adventure in the first place. Felicity glanced around to confirm to herself they were safe, quickly finding Techno's hand casually examining the contents of her coat pocket.

"What a bloody hoot!" Techno shouted as he neatly evaded Felicity's left boot, which was heading in the general direction of his backside. He said this in such a casual manner you'd think he was completely oblivious to the magnitude of what had transpired. He sat in his seat and fiddled with his recently liberated Gas Giant War-Pole. "I bloody bet I would have made a fine King of the Gas Giants."

"I bet you would have, Tech, I bet you would have," Nickolas laughed.

20. Dangerous Sun-Cycles

"I WOULD RATHER BE A RICH FOOL THAN A DEAD HERO"

The operational lights on the *Aletheia* flickered back to life, as Sama1tha was again able to direct her run-time back to her own ship.

"Did the Milarum's escape?" Thomas asked. He'd been waiting in almost complete darkness for the power to return.

"1t was a close call, and 1 am sure your father will b3 R3ALLY wrapped if he ever f1nds out. But, yes, they r cl3ar and currently 1n tachyon-space." Sama1tha couldn't have given the phrase 'close call' a more accurate meaning if she'd tried.

"Great work. Thank you, Sam," Thomas replied, with more than a hint of relief in his voice. "Now let's pay my father a visit, shall we? I think he has some explaining to do."

***

"What the blasted heck happened out there, sonny boy?" Franklin asked Thomas who, by courtesy of his family's 'home-in-a-hurry' transport devices, was safely seated in Franklin's office[104].

"I was going to ask you the same thing. Most of our fleet were blown away by these Zarnegy jokers. They possessed more firepower than my sister's vocab after a long night-cycle on the turps. Even when they were cloaked, they possessed firepower, which isn't possible."

---

[104] One of only two in the entire Galaxy. This single person destination jump device comes in handy when your supper's going cold, or you've forgotten your partner's birth-cycle party.

"It is for them."

"I knew it," Thomas said angrily. "What you're saying is you knew all along the Zarnegy were going to show up."

"Yes, of course. It was me who told them where the Milarum's were. I've been in communication with them for some time."

"You must have missed the bit about friendly fire, because they blasted half of *our* ships, without even saying a word." Thomas by this time had healed his leg by his ship's med-e-lab but was still feeling a little sorry for himself.

"Yes, that isn't ideal I admit."

"Isn't ideal? You're joking, right? These associates of yours don't care about anything or anyone, from what I've seen. They would probably blow away their own grandmother, given half a feeble excuse. Why do they want this Amulet so badly?"

"Oh, they don't care about the Amulet. They promised it to me, if I assist them. They want the Collector of Octarma, nothing else."

"What? That Xymod character?"

"Yes. If they can destroy him, then it's game over."

"So, what's in it for us? Why should we help them destroy half our own galaxy, while they track this Xymod character down?"

"Because they don't want to destroy it. They only want to control it. With the Octarma out of the picture, they will control the entire universe. Obviously, good business contacts to have long term, wouldn't you say? However, while this Xymod character lives, and if he collects the other Shards and fuses them into the Amulet, then he will be a threat, and they can't afford for that to transpire, for obvious reasons."

Thomas shook his head. "Mad. The whole damn lot of you.

I know one thing for sure. If these valued allies of yours even so much as look funny at another one of our troops, then they'll have me to answer to."

"I will have words with them. In the meantime, we need to locate the Milarum's. They will be in hiding by now. Nonetheless, they must travel to another Octarma planet soon enough. Dispatch all our agents and spy drones. We need to find them and this Xymod character immediately."

"Okay, but I have a bad feeling about this, father. Why do I get the distinct impression we're being played for fools?"

"I would rather be a rich fool than a dead hero," Eloise interjected, as she entered the room, obviously already tuned into the current conversation. "Think of a galaxy with a few less Milarum's in it. Couldn't be a bad thing, could it?"

Thomas was beginning to think he wasn't so sure, although, he did have a laugh when Eloise's hologrammatic son, Timmy, sprang from out of nowhere, attached himself to her leg and shouted, "Mummy! Mummy!"

***

Gwendolyn and Romeo filed into Captain Bullet's office, back at QLEB headquarters. A hive of activity had erupted since they were last there. The captain's office was strangely quiet though when they closed the door behind them. Roberto sat in his usual chair, at his usual desk, with his usual half-drunk bottle of cheap cognac within reaching distance.

"You're both in one piece, I see?" His tone implied that he almost wished they weren't.

"Luckily forrr us a police patrrrol scout ship picked us up in nick of time. Someting about a favourrr it oved to some oter ship," Gwendolyn said.

"Oh, goody gumdrops." The captain took a mouthful of

cognac directly from the bottle. "Now we've confirmed *you're* okay, would you like to know how things are going on our end?" He said in a tone more patronising than the famous story of Boogo Loogo of Pertion 38[105].

"Sure-BEEP-BEEP," Romeo replied. Given his electronic origins, he wasn't picking up the true vibe of the conversation thus far. What he had picked up again was his e-tick.

"So, my all-star recruits, let me fill you in. After you two hot shots were ordered to execute a simple find and extract exercise on the lovely, harmless planet of Aertion 12, I find out instead you became mixed up in some sort of Gas Giant genocide business …"

"But—" Gwendolyn tried to interject.

"… which somehow started a chain reaction. Which! Not only led to the destruction of an entire fleet of the visHamogus finest troops and ships, but has somehow also triggered the reappearance of an ancient, long since extinct power…"

"But—" Gwendolyn tried again.

"…who before they disappeared, destroyed most of the rest of the planet and a small group of QLEB ships sent to investigate. As if that's not all, it has also come to my attention that you assisted the escape of the suspects you were sent there to 'find and extract'."

"Actually—"

"Now, is there anything else I should know? Maybe for the

---

[105] On reviewing his staff's performance during the company's annual employee review period, Boogo Loogo took the creative approach of describing his underachieving staff with sarcastic phrases such as, "Yeah, she is so wonderful," and "he is so upper management material." It's a crying shame his performance reviews were totally lost in translation by People and Culture, as shortly afterwards his incompetent staff ended up being promoted ahead of him. The moral here is simple: Never trust anyone who goes by the name Boogo Loogo. You're only asking for trouble.

second act you could simply firebomb the office and put what's left of your colleagues out of their misery once and for all. The same colleagues who are currently running around trying to clean up your mess," he said, gesturing to all the activity behind them.

"Ve can explain everrryting," Gwendolyn said calmly.

"Can you?"

"Yes … actually … No." Gwendolyn had a hard time believing what they'd witnessed, so thought the best strategy was to keep her mouth shut and live to fight another sun-cycle.

"Maybe this will jog your memory? I received a voice message from a certain Captain Harold Booting of Aertion 12, moments before his headquarters was completely disintegrated when a visHamogus battle cruiser crash-landed directly on top of it. Do you want to hear it?"

"Certainly. Accommodating-gentleman-even-if-his-diet-wasn't-what-it-could-be-BEEP-BEEP."

"I don't think his diet is the biggest of his problems now," Roberto snapped as he pressed play on the transmission.

"Dear valued colleagues . I am not sure what constitutes a 'keep out of trouble' warning on your planet but considering the chaos you have unleashed by 'pissing in my pool,' rest assured, when I catch up with you, I am going to take great pleasure in ripping you both a new—"

Bbbeeeeeeeppppppp: Transmission Lost.

"Anything else you'd like to share? Maybe something has rattled free from those selective memories of yours?"

"Nope. Still nothing," Gwendolyn said with a guilty cringe.

"In that case, this is what you two are going to do. You're going to get up, get the hell out of my office and what the hell I ordered you to do in the first place. Oh, and don't come back until you have the *entire* Milarum family with you—"

"But—"

"I don't care if you have to wheel out a bunch of 200-lunar-cycle-old, long-lost relatives from every second retirement village in the galaxy. If they have the surname Milarum, then I want a few words with them. Understood?"

"Yes-Sir-BEEP-BEEP."

"And if you disobey another of my orders, I will take great pleasure recommending to high command we use those flea bag joints you call 'fine dining establishments' as target practice for our next round of deep space combat manoeuvrers. Understood?" Bullet pointed at the door. "Dismissed!"

"Oh, and one last thing. You can drop by the hospital and pick up that security guy, Charlie Quinkydink, or whatever his name is. Apparently, he pulled through his mental breakdown and is eager to assist in this investigation any way he can."

"Fan-fking-tastic," Gwendolyn said simply.

After Gwendolyn and Romeo had left his office, Roberto put the cap back on his bottle of cognac and carefully slid it into his top drawer. He also took out his QLEB standard issue ConVoser-6 laser pistol, and after a few, long, contemplative moments said, "It's times like these I remember exactly why I still practice law enforcement. It's being able to serve out rough justice to any invading scumbag in the galaxy and get paid for it."

21. The Zarnegy

"QURKITION, HUH? NEVER HEARD OF IT."

Grand Archduke Zarc of the Zarnegy sat in his colossal black chair, in his private quarters, on the largest of the four Zarnegy War-Citadels. His ship was now re-cloaked and moving with great pace back to their temporary base on one of the planets in the Outer-Brim. "So, dee ship escaped?" he enquired.

"Yes, my Archduke," Admiral Fluzzy, his second-in-command, replied. Fluzzy looked more than a little bit worried about his future existence prospects.

"Dee ship vas protected by a powerful spell. And zey somehow repaired zeir lightspeed drive and fled before ve could destroy it."

"It surffiffed a direct hit by one of our Var-Citadels. Impressive," the Archduke replied.

"Dee Octarm Amulet do you zink Archduke?" Fluzzy asked.

"I doubt it. As you know ve'ffe been down zis paff many times before. All paffs ending up a vaste of time. Neffertheless, haffe Countez Vipc and her Black Mist scan dee planet again and unleash dee Mortema Vatch[106] to dee surface to investigate."

"Zose crazy zealots? Zey are as liable to butcher our own troops zan to azist us."

"Zey're a pazionate bunch to be sure. But once ve haff communicated vhat ve might haffe found here, zey vill insist on being inffolffed. So best to utilise zeir skill set to our adffantage.

---

[106] The Mortema Watch major character traits: 50% Zarnegy religious zealot who uphold the sadistic scripts of 'The Word of Victarm' to the letter and 50% heavily armed troll-type creature with below average intelligence and itchy trigger fingers. = 100% Intergalactic Bastard!

Zat's a good man," the Archduke said.

"As you command. I vill inform zeir High Priestez immediately," Fluzzy replied, all the while thinking that even in his darkest moments, he would not wish those cutthroat religious nutters on anyone, including his greatest enemy.

"And if ve find zat it is dee Stevard of the Octarma and zat ship vas in fact protected by dee Amulet of Octarm? Should ve contact high command?"

"No. Let's inffestigate zis further before ve inform anyone outside our command. Especially High Lord Parc. I owe her no faffours anyvay. She has pazed me up for promotion numerous times, dee old battleaxe. She vould be dee last person I vould vant to share dee glory vith. It is best to keep zis to ourselffes for now."

"But vat if it is, sir? After hundreds of solar-cycles searching dee unifferse for it, could it pozibily be it?" Fluzzy hissed.

"Zis is our time, make no mistake. For ve are dee Zarnegy, dee beloffed disciples of Victarm, zis unifferse's true rulers. And ve vill search another billion galaxies in dee unifferse, if need be to find dee Octarm Amulet and Shards. And once acquired, dee entire unifferse vill bow at our feet," the Archduke bellowed, by now fully off topic, in a bigger and louder voice than was necessary.

"It vill be a glorious cycle indeed," Fluzzy replied in a slightly confused tone. He looked around the room expecting to see an audience.

"A glorious cycle indeed. I like zat, Fluzzy. I might use zat myself. So, vhat do you zink of dee opening of my ffictory speech? Not too forced or clichéd? I am zinking of using it to open my next public speaking engagement." The Archduke had a habit of practising his impending speeches on his underlings.

"I am sure you vill haffe dee audience eating out of dee palm of your hand," Fluzzy said.

"You're too kind, Fluzzy. Let's hope you don't fail me again. Zat's a good man. I quite like our little chats, and vould hate to haffe to terminate you in front of dee entire crew leaffing me vith dee unpleasant task of informing your family. Vich, as you know, vill be somevat awkward, and you know hov I dislike unpleasant situations."

Fluzzy looked nervous. "Yes, sir. I vill try and not put you in one. Consider it done."

"Zat's dee spirit. Now go now find zat ship. Zat's a good man. If it truly is dee Octarm Amulet, I vant it and all dee Octarma neutralised immediately. Pull vhatever zis galaxy's name is apart if you need to. And inform visHamogus ve require zat secret project he has been vorking on for us to be fully operational immediately."

"Qurkition, sir"

"Qurkition?"

"Dee name of zis galaxy is Qurkition, sir."

"Qurkition, huh? Never heard of it. Silly name for a galaxy if you ask me. About as menacing as a name as yours, Fluzzy, no offence meant of course. Zat's a good man." The Archduke laughed.

"Yes, sir. Very silly," Fluzzy said, taking great offence, but at the same time edging closer to the exit, and, in his mind, to freedom.

"Oh, and Fluzzy?

"Yes, sir?"

"I vill see you later for supper, right?" The Archduke swivelled his immense chair around, and looked out at the stars from his command centre window. All the while he held some sort of model spacecraft[107] in his hand, examining it closely.

"Oh, of course, Archduke. Looking forward to it."

Fluzzy didn't know what was worse: the constant threat of execution hanging over his head; having to sit through another night-cycle with the Archduke; or paying attention while he practised more lines from his impending 'universal speaking tour.'

---

[107] Although the Zarnegy were an aggressive race, they had two quite unexpected passions: public speaking and model making. Most Zarnegy agreed that giving an opening keynote address at a model making conference was the highlight of their entire lives.

22. The Animus

"IT'S ABOUT TIME SOMEONE WAS HAPPY TO SEE US."

The *Beletheia* dropped out of tachyon-space after what felt like a lifetime to the crew. In reality, it had only been a few moments.

"There are more than a few questions I have for you, M011y. However, for now, I'm glad we're all safe," Felicity said, with relief in her voice.

Nickolas casually pointed out of one of the bridge's observational screens. "I'm not sure I would consider 'safe' being right in the flight path of three comets. But you do you."

Everyone turned. Nickolas was right. Three large comets were on a collision course with the *Beletheia*. They were travelling at such an extraordinary speed that the *Beletheia* had no chance to take evasive action.

"Brace for impact!" Nickolas shouted. He threw himself, Nerada and Techno to the floor.

The impact never came. The lead comet flew straight at them, but instead of destroying the *Beletheia*, they found themselves gently guided into the middle of a huge hangar, which was built into the comet itself.

Felicity winked at Xymod.

"Now, now my fearless Protectors." Felicity said, looking amusingly at the sprawling bodies of Nickolas, Techno, and Nerada. "This does reek of amateur-cycle. I hope every time you're faced with a hopeless situation you don't simply close your eyes, hit the floor, and hope for the best. Now open your eyes, and I'll show you what your inheritance has been spent on. Welcome everyone, to the *Animus*."

The *Animus* was a large and impressive military complex, constructed deep within an icy comet. It had been built, sparing no expense, using the finest materials and latest technology available. It was able to support some 100,000 troops, and thousands of ships. The hangar the *Beletheia* had landed in was so large it could quite possibly match the size of Charlie Queerodon's ego[108].

The most impressive feat however was the advanced engineering that allowed short-time manual navigational control over the three comets via 30,000 strategically placed hyper-engines.

The companions disembarked the *Beletheia*. Their facial expressions were confused and resembled those of a young child who has seen a magic trick performed for the first time. Not by the Milarum twins mind you, but by real, qualified, and award-winning children's entertainers. To their even greater surprise, they were greeted with loud applause by what looked like a small army of troops. Many handshakes, high fives, and random hugs followed.

Jonathan, the last to disembark, touched the hull of the *Beletheia*

"Thanks, old girl … for everything."

M011y sensed the emotion in his voice. "Remember th1s th3 next time u try and pass 0ff som3 non-genu1ne parts as leg1t dur1ng my upcoming annual serv1ce."

He smiled guiltily, "Oh, yes, indeed."

Nerada glanced at Nickolas. "It's about time someone was happy to see us. Even if I don't know any of them from a bar of Eoop[109]."

---

[108] Not possible you think? Then you should see the impossible size of this hangar!

[109] Cheap soap, and I mean cheap.

Techno obviously didn't care. He returned handshakes, high fives, and pleasantries with anyone who came within pickpocketing distance. He then regaled his captive audience with personal tales. Though, given the background noise, the companions didn't get many of the details. They all assumed that whatever he was saying was an impressive work of fiction. Two tall women dressed in pure white flowing robes appeared and approached Xymod. They knelt before him, and Xymod gestured for them to stand, before replying to them in a strange language — the same language he had spoken with his brother. Looking pleased, he then turned to the companions. "Thank you, my Protectors. I couldn't have done this without you. However, there is much work to be done. I will have my assistants commence your training immediately."

"Training for what?" Nickolas asked. "If you hadn't noticed, Techno and I are already the perfect finished article in intergalactic heroism."

Nerada and Felicity shook their heads in exasperation.

"Training to harness your gifts," Xymod continued. He gestured at the necklace hanging around Nickolas's neck. "This, is no two-bit trinket. It is now the architect of your destiny. If used correctly, a Steward of Octarma necklace will give you immense power. Used incorrectly or without control …"

Everyone's eyes automatically fixed on to Techno.

"Oh, this gets better and better. I don't know what's worse," Nickolas said sarcastically, "that we now have a Zarnegy bullseye painted on our backs, or I have to pitch up to some sort of boot camp for the magically challenged."

Felicity looked at Xymod. "Forgive my brother. He was dropped many times on the head as a baby, toddler, and as a small child. Of course, we will all be ready for your training. It will be an honour."

Xymod nodded, and then swiftly retired to his quarters, with his entourage in tow.

Felicity's two furry companions, who she had sent ahead to prepare for their arrival, approached and welcomed her, with Matilda jumping onto Felicity's shoulder. Felicity then led the companions to the main control centre, within the heart of the comet.

"We will all be safe here," she said. "And given the speed we're travelling; we'll be almost impossible to track."

A short, thin female, who looked a great deal like Gwendolyn, and who was obviously a Coovet, came forward and saluted Felicity. She then whispered a few things into her ear.

"Thank you, Commander Philyn. May I introduce my brothers, Jonathan and Nickolas. This Fizbot here is Prince Techno. And you already know my sister, Nerada."

Grrreetings, my Gakusei," Philyn said to Nerada. "I look forrrvarrrd to continuing yourrr trrraining vhile you arrre herrre."

Nerada bowed slightly. "Thank you, Sensei."

"Now I know why she can jolly well handle herself in a scuffle," Jonathan said. He had heard about the legendary hand-to-hand fighting prowess of the Coovet.

"Impressive little operation you have, sister," Nickolas said. He looked around at the massive enterprise Felicity had put together. "Planning on starting a war, are you?"

"In our line of business, you always need a fallback plan. One out of the prying eyes of the public."

Nerada laughed. "What? In children's entertainment?"

"Laugh all you want," Felicity said, "but as you can see, this fallback plan pretty well much got us out of the kiifa[110] and gives us the perfect hideaway while we plan our next move."

"Yes, indeed," said Nickolas, who was still looking around curiously at his new surroundings. "It's almost as if someone has been prepping this contingency plan for some time now."

"That may be so. Nevertheless, I don't give a stuff how we arrived at this point," Nerada said. "I'm more interested in the plan from here. Hopefully, it's a plan which doesn't involve me getting vapourised."

"The plan is simple," Jonathan said. "Now we ruddy well go after the second Shard, then the third, like our father requested. We've started a chain of events here, and if we don't finish our quest and destroy the Zarnegy, I fear not for the safety of our galaxy but of every galaxy."

At this the room went quiet, and everyone nodded in agreement.

Jonathan himself felt different. Something had changed in him over these past few cycles. He felt more focused, more determined than ever to help locate the Shards and find out the whereabouts of his father. All the cycles of drifting around, of keeping his brother out of trouble now felt like a waste of time. The other possibility is he just needed to get a grip and have a few stiff drinks.

"Hold that thought," Nickolas said, as if he were reading Jonathan's mind. Nickolas signalled Techno with his eyes. "Not before we have a nice piece of banana cake and a few wind-down cocktails, we won't. Priorities, after all."

"Wind-down?" Felicity said with a funny look on her face. "Are you seriously telling me that 'winding down' would imply that you two reprobates got wound up in the first place?" She

---

[110] An uninteresting variant of a pickle.

removed Techno's hand from her back pocket and retrieved her credit chip from him before it disappeared into one of his mega-pockets. "No, you don't. You two intergalactic heroes can buy your own drinks. Meteor Space-Stations don't pay for themselves, you know."

"Oh, you and your jolly, playful banter," Jonathan said. He grabbed Nickolas, Felicity and Nerada and gave them all a big family hug, which they all immediately recoiled in horror from.

"I'm sure everything will work out spiffingly. We will find father soon; locate the other Shards; save the galaxy; and, who knows, maybe even by golly gosh get Nickolas a date along the way."

"Now that would be a miracle," Nerada said. She grabbed Techno by the hand and along with her brothers headed towards the largest bar, on the dirty ice block they now called home.

Felicity opened a communication channel with the *Beletheia* "Now, M011y, before I catch up with Xymod, a few answers from you, my little high-roller super-computer."

23. Does Nickolas Milarum Dream of Universal Peace?

"OH-WHAT-A-HERO-BEEP-BONK!"

Felicity entered Nickolas's sleeping quarters and found him face down and passed out on his bed. It was still early-night-cycle, but, according to Jonathan, Nickolas had challenged the off-duty Commander Philyn to a drinking contest[111]. As Felicity removed a bunch of Nickolas's things strewn all over a chair and sat down, the result was plain to see.

She had a mountain of work to do, and as she typed feverishly on her e-tablet, she listened with slight amusement as Nickolas, in-between some heavy snoring, loudly sleep-narrated his latest dream:

Oh, golly gosh, everyone, Gwendolyn cried, what with being locked in this impregnable cell and the entire prison wired with explosives about to blow, we will need real hero to save us!

Don't worry, my damsel in distress. I will save us, or my name isn't Nickolas 'Muck-a-muck' Milarum.

Oh-what-a-hero-beep-bonk! said Romeo. How can you possibility break us out of here, big man? It's impossible!

Nickolas took iNegotiat from his pocket. With this! he said. He then dropped it on the floor, crushed it with his boot and picked a few bits and pieces out from the debris.

Oh-what-a-hero-beep-bonk! Romeo said in awe.

---

[111] Other than possessing superhuman strength, the Coovet also possessed a strong tolerance to anything alcoholic.

Stand back, everyone! Nickolas fused a few of the crushed iNegotiat components with some chewing gum and hot-wired the holding cell door, which immediately swung open.

Quick! This way, everyone! He disabled one prison guard, while simultaneously shooting six others.

Please save us, hero! Shouted the other prisoners, who all happened to be attractive females.

Never fear, ladies, for I am here!

Nickolas pressed some random button, and the rest of the prison cells swung open.

Oh-what-a-hero-beep-bonk! Romeo repeated in awe … again.

Let's blow this joint!

Nickolas and the prisoners burst through the exit door and found themselves on the edge of a high cliff.

Gwendolyn held Nickolas close. The only way off this island is to jump into the ocean. We will never make it! She spoke.

Nickolas looked down the extremely rocky cliff face. Sure, we will, my pretty. I have seen worse.

Oh-what-a-hero-beep-bonk! Romeo repeated, who by now pretty much had the phrase on replay.

Good luck, everyone. Gwendolyn grabbed Nickolas and gave him a long, hard kiss. Boil me an egg. I will be back to crack it!

In the end, Nickolas 'Muck-a-muck' Milarum didn't have to negotiate the rocky cliff, as he was woken from his latest dream with a thud, as he fell out of bed and hit the floor headfirst.

Startled, he looked up at Felicity, who had a slight grin on her face.

"You're still having your entertaining night-cycle dreams so it seems. And who is this Gwendolyn girl?"

"How do you know that? And none of your business. And what the hell are you doing here?" Nickolas attempted to stand, bumped his head again, and sat back on his bed trying to soothe his injuries.

"There was a time I used to sit with you and Jonathan each night-cycle, if you remember?"

"Yeah, I remember," replied Nickolas who had to admit this was true. Felicity had often read to them in the night-cycle when they were young, especially after their mother had gone missing.

"You know what you did was extremely brave, Ni," Felicity said.

"What do you mean?" Nickolas hadn't heard his sister refer to him as 'Ni,' his childhood nickname, for some time.

"Going after the Shard like you did. Xymod told me the entire story. I'm proud of you. I know you and our father have never seen eye-to-eye, but what you and Techno did in the Gas Giants throne room was truly heroic. And your fancy trick to buy us more time while M011y repaired the tachyon-drive most likely saved our lives too."

"Not bad for someone who doesn't get wound up then," he replied sarcastically.

"Yes, well," said Felicity, now a little embarrassed over her previous comment.

"But alas, I haven't tagged along on this merry little adventure for our father. A father who still hasn't bothered to show up, I might add."

"So why are you here? You've had plenty of opportunities to leave."

"Well, someone has to keep an eye on Jonathan. He does seem to love these types of adventures a little too much. And now with Nerada, and obviously yourself, caught up in this, even though I could strangle you at times, it's my place to be here. What is that favourite phrase of yours again? Family first? So here I am."

"We can both agree on the strangling thing, Ni. But I'm glad you're here. You were always the smartest of us Milarum's. And I get the feeling we'll be relying on that intellect of yours fairly heavily before this is all said and done."

Nickolas looked down at his necklace. "It doesn't look like we have much choice now anyway."

"No, I guess you're right. Anyway, I had best be going. I'll let you get back to what seemed like an extremely entertaining dream. Oh, and your impending hangover, if the smell of this room is anything to go by."

"Impending no more, I'm afraid. I may already be feeling the effects of one-too-many cocktails."

Felicity stood and kissed Nickolas on his forehead. "Sweet dreams, brother," she said before she left his room.

Nickolas sat for a while and stared out of his quarters window as the comets approached the nearest sun at breakneck speed. Whatever they had got themselves mixed up in, he couldn't help but think that no matter how many swanky necklaces they got given, and how many fancy tricks they had up their sleeves, that the worst was yet to come. His family and friends were, in essence, very small cherries mixed up in the middle of some sort of universe-size cocktail.

"Thinking of cocktails, maybe one more for the road," he muttered as he grabbed his coat and went in search of Commander Philyn for a rematch.

***

As the controlled comets slung-shot their way around a nearby sun, they also launched numerous scout droids, whose function was to search the galaxy for intelligence on the Zarnegy, the visHamogus, and the latest slug race results from Omertion 6[112].

The last scout droid was launched in a completely different direction, out towards a solitary planet, which was situated on the other side of the galaxy.

This was a peaceful planet — a planet of great beauty. A planet that if it knew the trouble that was marching with great confidence in its general direction, it would most likely have packed its proverbial bags and made a run for the nearest wormhole.

***

Next Up ...

The Stewards of Octarma & The Fabulous Fun Kingdom Fantasy Land.

---

[112] Nickolas claimed that it was a matter of life or death.

About the Author

R H Polden currently lives in sunny Melbourne, Australia with his Bear, two adventurous fluff balls, and a subscription to Glamour.com magazine. He spends his spare time tinkering with technology and quoting/discussing (at length) insightful old Punk song lyrics with complete strangers at parties. Parties he has often not even been invited to.

For more information on his books, musical releases, and random ramblings about who knows what visit: polden.io

Acknowledgements

To the editorial team, Kim Smith and Peta Culverhouse, whose extensive knowledge of cocktail recipes is impressive. However, I do feel their inexplicable interest in the finances of a certain QLEB restaurant chain warrants some investigation.